GATE-CRASHING THE DREAM PARTY

ALISON LEONARD

WALKER BOOKS
LONDON

First published 1989 by Walker Books Ltd
87 Vauxhall Walk, London SE11 5HJ

This edition published 1990

© 1989 Alison Leonard
Cover illustration © 1989 Su Huntley/Donna Muir

Printed in Great Britain by Cox and Wyman Ltd, Reading
Typeset in Hong Kong by Graphicraft Typesetters Ltd

British Library Cataloguing in Publication Data
Leonard, Alison
Gate-crashing the dream party.
I. Title
823'.914 [J]   PZ7
ISBN 0-7445-1487-8

Chapter 1

And everyone famous was there – the Queen dragging Princess Anne in a pushchair, Paul McCartney looking like Lady Macbeth in a pink bikini. And I was the engine of it all. It was a merry-go-round with me as the central pole...

Well, that's it, then. The End. Curtains. The party's over.

Sitting on the train. Seat to myself. Headphones on my ears, deep into heavy rock, reading my dreams. The guard has to knock my elbow when he comes to inspect my ticket. My dreams are the only place where no one can touch me.

I'm on my way. Alone. Away.

I'm empty inside. They've gone, all those people who've been marching around inside my head: Mum, Dad, teachers, infuriating old Brian – even Cal who's everyone's friend when I'm nobody's friend but she's special to me...

Where to go? That'd been the big question. A city, to get lost in. Not Birmingham, too close, too obvious. London? Too far, too dangerous, too obvious. How about Bristol? Mum took us there yonks ago. What was that ancient ship she dragged us round? Gut-rottingly boring. Mum said it "smelt of history" and it did. I'd wanted to mooch round Bristol's hills and shops, its hidden alleyways and markets, along all those rivers. Great place, I thought – things actually happen here. Not like home. Only thing that happens at home is Course Work and Exams.

OK. Bristol – that'll do.

Shame I can't tell Cal. Well, if she will go off to Spain. She'd arranged with the school for me to see her results and report later when she phoned from the villa.

There was a rugby scrum outside the staff-room. I might've guessed the worst when the scrum fell apart for me like the Red Sea. God, was it that bad? Worse than my most fantastic nightmares? Not that I'd actually had nightmares about that. Everything but.

Did they know my results? How could they know? Someone said, "You're late, Beano." And someone else, "She'd be late for her own funeral."

Head in the air – they wouldn't dare call me "show-off" at a moment like this – I launched myself down that gaping passage-way and marched in to Dinwiddie's room.

A funeral – that's what last night's dream was. Whose funeral was it? I know whose. I was coming round the dream-corner and... *There I was. But it was another me. I was sitting upright in a pine coffin high on a marble pedestal and wearing a delicate silk gown of pure white. I turned towards one of the crowd, a grey hunched wrinkled old crone, and started arguing with her in formal fashion: was I dead, or was I not? All round us was a crowd of misty dream-people – though I'm in the crowd, too – milling and muttering, and they're looking at me in my silken gown and murmuring to each other, "Isn't it dreadful – Robina's dead! Such a lovely girl, and so clever!"*

Outside the open door, the crowd fell silent. Don't exaggerate, they were still whispering at the edges.

"Can I see Cal's results first, please?" Mrs Dinwiddie (Deputy Head, face square, lips pursed) handed over the envelope – Fry, Caroline Olga. (Olga! – she'd be mad that'd got out.) I pulled up the gluey flap. "I'm afraid I can't let you have Caroline's actual document, Robina." (Afraid – Dinwiddie?) "Just a glance, then give it back."

Cal's were: English Language, B. English Literature, A. Maths, C. Physics, B. Drama, A. Chemistry, C. And so on like that. Fair enough – Cal was fine. I put it carefully back in its envelope and gave it back to Dinwiddie, who slipped it into the pile.

"Fry – Kirby – MacDonald. Here we are – Marquis, Robina." (No Robina Mary, Robina Elizabeth for the girl who should have been a boy.) She passed it over. Silence.

Same gluey envelope – it wouldn't open – I tore bits off. Calm down, Bina, it'll be OK – magic, I'll have shot through the lot – straight As, I'll be all set for anything: research physicist, brain surgeon, professor of semiotic philology…

This dream I'm reading now – I dreamt it when we were at the cottage in Cornwall. (Dad wasn't there. Dad can't manage holidays.) July 7th. *A lake. Somewhere like Switzerland – peaky mountains with snow on top, glaciers… But I'm in the lake, I'm floating on my back in the water. The sun's hot and I've got no clothes on. The lake's full of people – Mum wearing her Interviewing suit – Brian with knobbly knees under his grey schoolboy shorts – Gran in her Margaret Thatcher blouse – but they don't bother me, they don't bump into me. Then I turn over and put my face under the water, and I can see that they're all floating just under the surface of the water. Don't they need to breathe? No, and I don't either. Are we all dead? All this death! How about that, Mr Freud? I can see Dad in a black suit and tie – even a black waistcoat with three black buttons – and he looks deadest of all. I've opened my mouth and I'm singing a Beatles song – which one? "Yesterday – All my troubles seemed so far away – Now I need a place to hide away, Oh – I believe in Yesterday."*

No I don't (believe in Yesterday). Yesterday was Home, Them, Grades. Today's what matters. Going's what matters. Leaving "my" room – what was mine about it? Jolly poster of skiing in the Alps stuck up by Mum as a bribe: "Ten days in Austria if you get Grade As, Bina!" Certificates for flute and swimming hung up on strings by Dad. Even the pop posters were old, they blew my mind with boredom. My duvet: I'd really miss my duvet, it's my friend. And the video-tape of Cal and me playing Bottom and Titania in *A Midsummer Night's Dream* last year, with us collapsing in giggles when she tripped over a cobweb and brought down half the lights.

Then there's a fuzzy bit I can't remember – *oh yes, it's not a lake, it's the sea, with tremendous waves, and I'm still on my front looking downwards, but the people have disappeared, and the sea's full of the furniture at Cal's house – the grandfather clock that chimes every quarter hour, the gold velour sofa, all those tiny thimbles and china bells that her mum dusts every day of her life, even their bath and loo in trendy slate-blue – and everything is swirling round as if a great Sea God was stirring it like a pot full of stew.*

Lakes. Sea. Drowning. Meaning – just what?

Where's the scruffy page I tore out of that magazine at the dentist's? Search for it through the wodge of bits of paper and exercise books and writing pads that my dreams, all my precious dreams are scribbled on. Here – unfold it, straighten it out: YOUR DREAMS CAN TELL THE MEANING OF YOUR LIFE. Birds (in cage, clipped wings) – you're inhibited! Teeth (falling out) – fear of old age… Ah! Water: another of those symbols of anxiety. Are you playing victim again?

Oh yes, dear magazine, I was a victim. But not any more. Things are going to be different now.

I sit back. I fancy a cup of coffee from the buffet, but I'll have to be careful with money.

Been to the cash dispenser, got a statement, then withdrawn everything except four pounds ninety-five to keep the account open. So I've got eight crisp ten pound notes and one five pound note. That's eighty-five pounds less my rail fare. I was saving for Austria – even banked all my birthday money in May. That should see me for a while.

A while. A little while on my own. And then? Don't ask.

It had happened. I'd got them: Fs, Gs, and the Big U – Unclassified.

Dinwiddie was saying – pretending to comfort, actually furious. "We're querying it, of course – "

I read: English Language, F. English Literature, G. Maths, U. Physics, U. Biology, G. History, F. French, U. Art…

"Your course work was patchy, but sometimes excellent. A freak result – nerves – you must have written gibberish. We've got the kettle on, I brought

11

in some milk to give soothing cups of coffee where necessary…"

"Piss off," I said. (Did I really? Or is that a dream as well?) "And don't strain yourself with querying. The lot of you can roast in hell."

You should've seen me marching home.

Past everyone, past the Brilliant Gang at the gates, I nearly knocked one of them over. It should have been raining, thundering, hailing. But no, the sun beat down, I'd have a tan to rival Cal's on the Costa Blanca.

I screwed up my results paper and threw it on the pavement beside someone's half-eaten chips on the corner.

Home. Open the door. "Hi…?" No one in, of course. Brian was Adventuring, scaling Junior Buttress or wobbling in a canoe, probably falling off or drowning. Mum off teaching at some distant Employment Training Scheme. Dad At Work at the bloody Theatre – where else?

I went straight upstairs and stood in the middle of my bedroom. What to take? My purple stripy barrel-bag – it was small, it'd look as if I was going off to my gran's for the weekend. I got it down from the top of the wardrobe. Would it fit my packet of dreams and some extra paper? I couldn't live without them. They were heavy: I'd have to wedge them in the middle so they didn't drag me down sideways.

Wash-bag. Make-up. Photo of Chris? I'd kept it in the bottom of my bra-and-pants drawer ever since I stole it from Dad. It was on a half-pasted-up Foyer Display on his desk at the theatre – Your Front-of-

House Man, Christopher Tomms – Dad must have raged at everyone to find it, but he never thought to ask me. I'd take the photo with me. No I wouldn't.

Not gel, too bulky. Alarm clock. Necessities – who knows how long I'd be away. Thick sweater, winter pyjamas not nightie, who knows where I'd be sleeping.

Away? Even then I didn't say the words: Leaving Home. For Good. For Ever. I just packed my things.

I'm reading the very first dream: *A ballroom, shimmering. Colours, shapes, moving in a dance – are they people, or ghosts? Chandeliers – so many of them, the room's like a river pool sparkling in sunlight. The room has no corners, no walls – it goes on for ever, it merges with a moonlit garden. I'm dancing with an enamoured Archduke. How do I know he's enamoured? Because he bows, lifts my lace handkerchief (sensitively dropped by yours truly) and returns it with a flattering smile. "Shall we dance?" And we move away, floating in time to the minuet.*

Hang on a minute – there's another me in the dream … *standing outside in the star-studded night. It's a cold, ragged, gypsy girl with filthy feet, and it's me. I can see the grime under my toenails, I can feel my hair hanging in greasy clumps. I'm shivering, unwashed and unhappy and unwanted. I'm not only shivering, I'm shrivelling away.*

The Robina who's dancing with the Archduke goes on dancing, whirling. Is it Chris I'm dancing with? Yes, it's the Archduke Christopher. But the other me, the gypsy, has fallen under the Evil Eye, and a shrill voice has pierced the air: Be accursed! Then I'm withering – shrinking – disappearing … I'm gone. All

13

that's left of me is a tiny cone-shaped pile of dust – and that's blown away by the whirling wind of the dance.

Down to the kitchen. Grabbed two packets of chocolate biscuits and a half-pound wedge of cheese. Apples? Too heavy. A packet of dried fruit. Drink? No, I could get water when I found a Ladies.

Back upstairs, I sat on the bed. OK I admit it, I was breathing heavily – panting. Leant back on my dressing table to calm down, clutched the handles.

Look around, I said to myself. Think what you're leaving.

My room should have been my own, my private space. But they were always barging in. "Busy, darling?" or "Turn that down, for god's sake!" Privacy's a myth in this house. Every creak announces what you're doing. I went for a midnight walk last February – it was snowing, I just got the urge, it was like a fairy tale, clean and soft – and they were standing in the hall when I got back, eyes frantic, fingers pointing, accusing me of – what? "Worrying us to death!" Not even, "Are you all right, darling?" I'd only wanted to be alone!

Alone now. People on the train – they're like ghosts, I can almost see through them.

What'll I do when I get to Bristol? Find a sunny park, lie and bask, read. I've left my books behind! Piles of books all over the floor: Agatha Christie, Dick Francis, P. D. James. I've done nothing but read thrillers since the exams, apart from watching videos and playing patience to kill time.

I knew I needed some place to go inside myself – frighten people off – so I shoved three tapes and my

14

Walkman in the middle of the bag beside the big fat envelope where I'd squeezed all my dreams.

I composed a note for them and left it in the hall beside the phone. Tore a piece of paper off the pad – then looked at the phone. Ring Chris, should I? He'd help me – he'd get me a job sweeping the stage at his new place...

Last time I'd phoned him – I felt sick remembering. "Motherwell Playhouse Theatre? Christopher Tomms? I'll see if he's in." A muffled laugh: "one more of Chris's cast-offs." "I'm sorry, he's not available. Can I give him a message?"

I lectured myself: No. Chris is over. Cal's away. You're on your own.

My note. Neatness, politeness – that'd lull them. "Got my results. I'm all right." (They'd read *They're* all right.) "Gone out. Don't wait up. R."

A PS: "When Caroline phones from the villa, tell her..." And I listed Cal's results, exactly. Nothing crappy about *my* brain.

Then, casually swinging my barrel-bag, off to the train.

The night before English Lit I had this utterly weird dream. *We were in this theatre watching* The Crucible *(no great significance about that, the Sixth Form had tried out their exam text on us) only they weren't on a stage, they were up on tight-ropes, and it was our job as audience to keep them up there, and we did that by holding our breaths. If any of us let go and started breathing again, one of them would fall off into a lake of mud. How d'you know the rules, in dreams? You just do. I watched with my breath held tight for what seemed like hours, but then I panicked, and let go. I*

15

felt relieved in the same huge way as when you've been desperate to pee and you finally get to a loo...

It's hot out there, out in the fields, in the sun. I'm sitting on the shady side of the train (dum-a-di-dum, dum-a-di-dum) but it's hot in here too. I'm parched – I'll die without a drink. Wait on, Beano, wait till you can get a free one.

And a woman fell off. She was dressed in one of those Puritan outfits for the play but she wasn't a Puritan, she was a nun. And because I'd let her fall off, she wouldn't be allowed to be a nun any more, because she had fallen into the lake of mud and I knew you couldn't be a nun unless your clothes were clean. And she wasn't an ordinary nun, she was... She was Mum. I could see her face now, Mum's face, eyeshadow and lipstick perfect as always, struggling there in the thick slimy mud – gasping, sinking... Then I wasn't in a theatre any more, I was...

Slowing down, pulling into Bristol Station. Shove my dreams and my Walkman back into the bag, and get off the train.

Chapter 2

Bristol Temple Meads. "What a name – quaintly medieval," Mum would say, educationally. Nothing medieval about the station: it was vast, fifteen times the piddling outfit at home. Vast as I'm feeling: like in a dream when you're walking naked down the High Street. I'm big, visible, vulnerable.

I strode over to the bookstall and bought myself a map of the place. Then I went to the Ladies and drank half a pint of water in little trickles in my cupped hands.

There were lots of other people in there, but I took no notice of them. I took my make-up out of my bag, leaned close to the mirror and set to work on my face.

When I came out not even Cal would have recognized me. I'd blacked my eyebrows till they were like tarmac, I'd put raspberry-coloured gloss thick on my lips and I'd done my eyelids in a limey shade of green. Black eyeliner on my lower lids, and I looked like some kind of She-devil. Gothic, almost.

Trouble was: if my face was Gothic, my hair should be Gothic too.

My gorgeous glossy dark locks used to be Mummy's Delight when I was little, but now it was just wavy like the sea at Brighton and I wore it long with a flyaway fringe – well, it was flyaway if I could stick it solidly enough with gel or spray. I couldn't stick it up at the back or I'd look aged, haggard, forty years old.

What would it cost to…?

Wow! I will! I'll have it cut. I'll wander round this place and find a cheapo hairdresser and I'll get it done – Gothic, or spiky, or something.

Walking out of the Ladies, I suddenly saw Mum's face in front of me like I saw it in the dream – sinking, drowning in bubbling mud – trying to spit the oozing slime out of her lipsticked mouth but the more she spat it out the more slithered in… It's amazing how detailed dreams are. More detailed than real life, more exact, more real. If I tried to picture Mum now like she really is, getting a Sainsbury's pizza out of the freezer in the kitchen or doing up the seatbelt of her silver Ford Fiesta, I couldn't. But I saw the sheen of her lipstick as she drowned in stinking slurry.

Then there was Mrs Dinwiddie. *And a bubble blew up under the mud, and when the bubble was as big as an elephant it burst, and out popped Mrs Dinwiddie. She looked even more head-mistressy than usual, a caricature, with a long black gown and a mortarboard that pressed down hard till it flattened the top of her head. Then she was blowing up like a bubble herself and getting fatter and fatter and more and more bulbous till she filled the whole sky and I knew that if she burst the explosion would drown me in mud too, and I could smell the slurry in my nostrils already and it was getting up my nose and I couldn't breathe and…*

Then I'd be dead. Big bad head-mistressy people making me dead: that's what lots of my dreams are about.

All that flashed through my head while I took one step out of the Ladies. Then, in a blink, the pictures of Mum and Mrs Dinwiddie and the sea of mud vanished, and I came out of that station floating six inches above the ground. I felt like flinging my arms about, twirling, leaping into an aerial somersault and landing back on my feet again.

I'm not dead. I'm alive. And I'm free.

No one knows I'm here. No one's watching me. No one wants to know how my character study of Mark Antony's going, whether I've vacuum'd under my bed, what videos I've been watching while they were out, how many lengths I've swum without a break, whether I'm telling the truth or lies. No one. No one! I'm alone. Me and me only. I've got money. I can do what I like.

A footbridge across a thundering ring road, and over it I found a shopping centre just like at home. There were a couple of smart hairdressers: one said, Restyling – this week only £12.50. A fortune! I'd have to strike out in a poorer direction. What was the time? 16.43. I'd better get a move on.

Bristol's all hills, I'd remembered that. The rivers: there was the Severn, but you don't see much of the Severn – and there's another one called the Avon, and lots of canals. There's no sea – I suppose you have to go along the estuary to find the sea.

I walked fast – my feet stood up to it very well, I'd been sensible and worn my trainers not my nice stiletto wobblers, but it still took me a fair old time to get to somewhere possible.

I began to see little old ladies clutching their pension books and garages called Krash Kare and Oxfam shops and Salvation Army hostels. There'd be a cheapo hairdresser around here.

At 17.23 I was sitting in Jake 'n' Suzi's Unisex Salon, a tiny place that looked as though

19

cockroaches'd run out of corners and over your toes. The girl with the scissors had a washed-out look, she'd probably got nits crawling under her blonde hair dye. She kept glancing at the massive Mickey Mouse watch that dangled round her thin bony wrist.

When she'd finished it was 17.31 and she almost pushed me out of the door. I came out, shorn, and my head felt cold. I'd closed my eyes while she was cutting so I couldn't see myself in the mirror. I hadn't even looked at the floor in case I got nostalgic for my own personal locks now lost to me for ever. The Mickey Mouse girl would be sweeping it all into the bin, along with any cockroaches she'd crushed underfoot.

Well, I'll have to find a place to lay my cropped and weary head for the night, won't I. This is the bit I've been trying not to think about.

Take a deep breath. Bed for the night. What kind of bed? Bed and Breakfast – that's for tourists. Am I a tourist? Glance at myself in a shop window: no. Go back for a second glance – is that really me?

I winked at myself, jiggled my head about, grinned. It wasn't Gothic, it was too short for that. But it was spiky. It looked much darker like this, almost black. Don't know about Cal not recognizing me, I hardly recognized myself.

Who am I? Not dear Julia's pretty little girl, or David's daughter who keeps hanging round the theatre, nor even Brian's big sister who'd lend the gang a quid for a video if they were skint. I'm not a fifth-former, or everybody's muggins when it comes to sorting out their Drama Practical, or an ace swimmer lately deteriorated, or a lapsed flute-player.

20

I'm nothing. Nobody. If I stood on a street corner somewhere, someone could slip me a small packet in exchange for a fiver and in a few hours I'd be slumped on the floor of a public toilet: a Drug Statistic. Then in a cold cell: a Crime Statistic.

At this rate I'll be a Homelessness Statistic.

A student! I could say I'm a student. I'll have booked in for a course in Bristol starting in September – an art course, no one cares what art students look like – or drama maybe. I'm eighteen (if they ask). My father's a refuse collector – or maybe an accountant or a barrister and I'm the rebel of the family.

Up and down a few more hills. The streets seemed to be getting narrower, the houses taller. People of all sorts of colours, shops selling chapattis and second-hand shirts. A policeman, white, talking to a gang of youths, black.

I went round another corner and took out the map to find out where I was, but it didn't help. What I wanted was an area marked "The sort of place where an average girl out on her own won't get mugged or raped and she can get a cheap bed for the night, no questions asked."

I was sweating now even though it was getting cooler. My shoulder ached – all those dreams. Why do I have to carry them around – why can't I just remember them? Because I need them, that's why. I need them written down, where I can touch them. They're the real me.

But I was hungry. No shops now. This looked more like flats and bed-sitters. It might be an area where… Yes! "B 'n' B. Rooms Vacent".

I pressed the bell. It did a Big Ben chime, and I

heard a chorus of kids' shouts from inside. The door opened, and there stood a boy of about ten, chewing gum and gawping. He said nothing. More kids appeared – half a dozen small pairs of eyes round about his waist, inspecting me. There was a pungent smell from along the hall and some dogs barking out the back. Or maybe wolves.

I managed to glare back at the boy, who went on chewing. We stood like that for ages, trying to stare each other out.

Then a stomping noise came from behind the kids and I saw some massive black rubber boots coming slowly down the stairs. Brown paint-streaked trouserlegs were tucked into the boots, and at the top the trousers ended in a scallop-shape where a hairy belly hung over in a loop, belly-button gaping. The belly wobbled as each boot hit a new stair.

Boots, belly and trousers got to the bottom. I looked up into a bloated quivering face with three days' growth of beard. Beads of sweat stuck out on his forehead and dripped in grimy trickles down his stubbly cheeks.

I coughed and said, "Good evening, I – " My voice sounded hoarse.

The man lifted up the paintbrush like a weapon. "Ceiling. Top floor. Purple, she said, for whatever fucking reason." His voice was amazingly soft – he almost cooed, in a country accent like telly-ads for butter. "You can't be the Gas, I s'pose you're the Room. 'Less you want some of me lead pipes." He giggled. The belly went into little convulsions.

"Yes. Is it – does it have a private bathroom?" I heard my fancy words, the posh accent.

And the man had a volcanic eruption. He turned into one massive enraged wobble. "Prive— ! You minx – you bloody whore…" The kids scarpered. "Fillet steak, that's what you'll be… I've Alsatians, six o' them, out the back… Get off my front step… Six of them, limb from limb they'll… You fucking—"

I ran. I was half-way down the road and he was still roaring. Is he coming after me?

Oh – oh – oh – I can hardly breathe – oh I can hear thumping – it's him, thumping after me…

No it isn't, it's my heart. I can't breathe – I'm sweating – my bag's banging on my hips and I'm getting bruised to bits – I've got to stop.

There was a little park – well, a few trees and some grass strewn with litter. I ran towards it and flopped on to an old bench. The back was broken and there was only one plank left to sit on, but I sat down on the peeling green paint.

Pant pant pant. Sweat soaking into my shirt, my jeans. Calm down, girl. He's not coming. He might – he might come and fling me on the grass and rape me. He won't. Set his Alsatians on me…

He won't. Calm down. Calm. Silence. Faraway traffic, a tiny breeze in the leaves above me. Silence. Sweat evaporating, coolness of wet cotton on my skin. Cool. Still. Alone.

My eyes begin to see again. There's a bench on the other side of the grass, and there's someone lying on it, sleeping on it. A bundle of coats in layers, with someone inside. The face is covered with hair, matted filthy hair like my gypsy hair in the dream. I think it's a woman. The hair isn't grey, it's dark brown like mine. It looks wet, but it can't be wet in this heat – it's the grease in it.

Down on the path beside her are a couple of brown bottles – I can't read the labels from this distance. Booze. No, meths. Meths – the stuff Bri uses in the shed to drive the little engines he makes. Now it's driving her. Killing her.

How old is she? Who were her parents? Did anyone love her once? Is anyone looking for her? Is it easy to get like her? How long till I get like her? How long before she gets eaten away by the meths and dissolves into dust blown by the wind? How long before I do?

I'm shivering. I'm scared. I'm alone. I want to cry, I want to comfort her, give her something, I want someone to give me something, comfort me.

I pick up my barrel-bag and fish around in it for my purse, take out a five pound note and walk over, rolling the note up in my hand. I'm going to fit it neatly into the neck of the one of the bottles. She'll only spend it on more booze and meths but I don't care.

I've just put the fiver in the bottle neck and I'm trying to get it to unfurl so it won't drop all the way down, when she groans. Instinct says – Run!

But a hand comes out and grabs me. She's got me by the jeans – the hand's scabby – she's got some skin disease. I pull away – but I can't run. I back away a bit, and kneel down. I'm still holding the fiver in the bottle because it bloody well won't unfurl.

I take it out and show it to her, move it towards her hand. "It's for you," I say. I feel like a priest giving someone Last Rites, only this priest wants to scream.

The hand shoots out again and grabs the fiver. I don't look at the face, only at the scabby hand. It clutches the note, screws it up and holds it to its greasy black coat. Nothing else moves. The body's asleep, drunk, inert except for the arm and the hand.

I stand up. I'm sick, drained. I walk back across the grass and pick up my barrel-bag. I keep my back turned. I've got to go, I've got to wash, I've got to find somewhere clean and decent to sleep, somewhere Mummy would approve of, fast.

Chapter 3

In kiddies' adventure stories they always wonder Where am I? when they wake up in a strange place. I always know where I am the instant I'm awake.

I'd found somewhere Really Rather Nice. She'd looked at me a bit strange, the woman in charge of the Bed-and-Breakfast, but I'd paid on the nail and ordered in my refined accent, "And a cooked breakfast, please" – so no hassle.

I was back on home ground. Laura Ashley wallpaper, hot and cold in all rooms and a clear fourteen pounds flown out of my purse. I couldn't do this again.

And I'd dreamt: *I was in a tiny dark shabby shop, something out of Dickens. There was dust everywhere – the shop was filled with a dense fog of it. The shopkeeper was a Hunchback of Notre Dame, twisted, with grotesque growths protruding from his body. But his face was beautiful – old and wrinkled – kind and calm and homely and wise – the perfect grandmother. He was making a kiss shape with his mouth, and when he made a kiss sound ... phut! all the dust disappeared.*

And the hunchback-grandfather was Dad, and the shop was an aquarium. On the shelves there were fish swimming in the air as if it was their natural habitat. There were sea-horses (always my favourite) and Dad said kindly, "Would you like one of the sea-horses? I'll serve it up on toast for you." Straightaway I could smell toast being made in the little room behind the shop among the scales and ledgers. I was just thinking it was very mean of me to have ordered sea-horse-on-toast for my tea … Or was that a half-waking thought? … when my alarm went.

Got dressed (glanced out of the window – hot again), made up (Gothic again), sat on the edge of the bed and took out my envelope of dreams and scribbled down last night's dream. *Hunchback… Dad… Sea-horse-on-toast…* Examined my hands – had I caught Scab Woman's scab? No.

Hope I'll be able to eat my expensive breakfast. In my bag I've only got… What? I took it all out, stroked each thing and put it back again. My worldly goods, my total possessions.

Walkman, alarm clock, my winter pyjamas (too hot, I'd thrown the duvet off in the middle of the night), my wash-'n'-make-up bag, and necessities. My dreams, and spare paper. Bra (one spare), pants (two spare), T-shirt, my white cotton trousers, purse with my bank card and rail card in, one-and-a-third packets of chocolate digestives (two-thirds eaten last night between Scab Woman and here), some cheese that had sweated fat and looked distinctly revolting, and the dried fruit.

What would I do when my clothes got dirty? There weren't any washing machines on the streets of Bristol. Oh, there are laundromats. Only they cost you. I've got to find a flat, and a job.

God, I was hungry.

Seven forty-seven by the clock. She'd said "Breakfast at eight." After breakfast: job-hunting. There'd be cafés, washing up, waitressing. Wait a minute – out of the corner of my eye at Temple Meads Station, when I'd blinked away the vision of Mum swallowing mud, I'd seen a sign on the window of the buffet: Vacancies. Should I try there?

I took my dreams down to breakfast: I'd scribble while eating, like an Inspector from the Good Bed-and-Breakfast Guide. Sure enough I got mushrooms and fried bread as well as bacon and egg and tomato, and porridge beforehand.

Before the sea-horses. Running – breathing hard – I'm in a tunnel. The air seems to dry up – I can't breathe – I'm being bounced, beaten up by nothing. There's something – someone – flying towards me. It's flying fast but approaching incredibly slowly – it's pressing itself towards me and waving and kicking so that I'm getting bruised all over. The thing that's flying towards me is multicoloured – I'm being beaten up by colours – grass-green violet scarlet beige BANG rust indigo lime BANG! rose-pink slate-grey flame-orange BANG BANG! – and the colours have got my face. I'm being beaten up by a jumbled-up rainbow-coloured ME.

And I could hardly force down my fourth slice of toast and marmalade. This grub would set me up for forty-eight hours at least.

I'd stuffed my little folded-up square of Dream Interpretations in my jeans' pocket. Took it out, unfolded it. Wind – nothing. Colours – each colour means something different. Hunchbacks – nothing there, either. What about Benevolent Old Man? Ah - Kindly grandfather/grandmother: another of Jung's "archetypes". Don't worry, s/he's your friend. Dad, my friend? Pull the other one.

"On holiday, are you?" asked the woman as I handed

28

in my key. She was motherly, with a big mole on her upper lip. Late forties, husband left her for younger woman most likely. Should I phone home? Say "I'm alive" and slam the receiver down?

"Just stopping off, actually," I said. "I've got an hour or two to fill in before my train. Could you direct me to that old ship – what's it called? – they dragged it up out of the —"

"The SS *Great Britain*? It's quite easy to find – just go down the road by the river – no, not towards the station, the other way – it's only a mile or so. On your way to somewhere nice, are you?"

Quick – sign the register, get out, escape from the puzzlement in her eyes.

It was hot, even as early as this. There'd be breezes by the river – I could sit and think, read my dreams. Or should it be the station first, see about that job? Wisdom before leisure, Beano. Money before dreams.

The station was only round a few corners – I must have walked round in circles the day before. The Vacancies notice was still up. If there are any tramps in there, I'm ignoring them.

Now, let's get our act together. Who should I be? Sweet little dairy-maid who'd enchant the customers but give them all the wrong change? Doesn't fit my Gothic. Sullen but accurate, spiky but efficient: that's it.

I went inside. "Excuse me, I've come about the job." Voice not too loud – soften the shock of my looks. The counter-girl told me I'd have to wait for the manager. He took about sixteen hours to come, and when he did come (tall and spindly and ginger haired) all he said was, "From the Job Centre, are you? I might

29

as well take your details."

Details? Why can't he just interview me, ask my experience as a waitress? I've got three stories ready.

"Name, sweetheart. Address. Where you live."

In a split second I knew what I'd done. I'd signed Robina Marquis and my full address in the signing-in book at the B 'n' B. The mole-woman might at this very moment be ringing Directory Enquiries to get the Marquis number and find out my story was all lies.

"Smith," I said to Spindly Ginger-Nob. "Mary Smith."

"Mary – Smith." His hand, freckly with light ginger hairs on it, wrote laboriously. "Address?"

My act vanished. I ran.

Got far away and my breath back and said, "Bina you silly cow, you should have said, 73 Severn View, Montpelier, Bristol." But no, my thought-processes paralysed – I panicked.

I'm on a roller-coaster. One minute I'm skyscraper-high: which of the exciting variety of Robinas will I offer the station buffet as their dazzling new waitress? – name your part, Bina'll shine at it, I only have to waltz in and offer my services and they'll fling open their arms in welcome.

Then – jump into the deep dark pit, Beano. You haven't got what it takes.

Back beside the ring road and the footbridge. Same as yesterday, and where had I got? Sweet nowhere.

All I'd got was my dreams. Nearly three months' worth of them – nothing before that – then, as soon as exams began: every single night I had them, and every single morning I wrote them down. I woke up early, woke naturally during that exam time. I never needed the alarm clock or Mum or Bri to hammer on my door. I told Mum that one day, to stop her nagging me about revising. "I'm sleeping well, and I'm waking on time, so I must be feeling confident." (I was still late for every exam, but I didn't tell her that.) I suppose I believed in magic. Thought my erratic Course Work'd see me through, or my papers'd get mixed up with someone else's who's a genius.

Especially I'd got my comfort-dream. *I was lying on a bed of colours. The colours were rose-petals that lay so light on my skin they were hardly there. I stretched out my whole body into the petals so that every square millimetre of my skin was softly touched, I wiggled my fingers and toes among the sweet perfumes ... and I was being embraced.*

I wasn't afraid. Those arms were my arms – even though my arms were still lazily resting among the rainbow petals. I was being embraced by someone safe – by me.

So I'd stay calm. I'd go to the SS *Great Britain* and sit by the breezy river, and I'd compose my stupid self and compose my story so that I could tell lies confidently instead of giving myself away. I needn't be frightened of the mole-woman: she'd be too busy making beds and totting up last night's proceeds to wonder whether I was a truant from a Youth Custody Centre or a prostitute on an overnight break.

Only, first I'd phone home. 10.07, Mum'd be up by now. Oh no – it wasn't a weekend, it was Friday, she'd be working.

But I had to phone. I had to tell her I was in Heckmondwike or Herstmonceaux, in case the mole-woman got in first. Then they wouldn't find me, and

I could plan my life and find a job and a flat and go home in six months' time having proved I'm adult and they'll have to let go and let me do what I absolutely, passionately want to do with my life. Which is?

First phone box vandalised. Second: four people in a queue outside. Third: dog-shit all over the floor. Fourth one smelt of sick, but it'd have to do. In any case if they weren't in after three rings I was giving up.

Mum'd be there, she couldn't go to work with this anxiety hanging over her. I'd worked it out to the last breath. As soon as she picked up the receiver I'd say, "It's Robina," and then cut off. Nothing more. No contact – just information. It'd keep them calm, stop them lying awake at night.

I dialled, waited, then counted the times it rang. Da-da... one. Da-da... two. Da—

"Yes?" It was Dad!

"Dad! You're not at work!" Oaf-twit-blockhead! You sound as if you ... care!

I could hear his intake of breath. "Robina!" He called away from the phone, "Julia – quick – it's her!"

I slammed down the receiver.

God, I was sweating. Dad, taking a day off work! Generalized panic at the Marquis' residence – hey, but that's something! Panic, for little ol' Bean!

They'd try and find me. Could they trace the call? The police wouldn't help, there were millions like me every year – well, thousands. In any case, I was sixteen, legal age for being on my own. Unless the mole-woman...

Where would they think I'd gone to? London – everyone thinks everyone goes to London. They'd imagine me prostituting myself, or on the hard stuff. They'd tell their friends I'd had "some kind of breakdown" or invent "boyfriend trouble" for me. Not that I'd told them about Chris, but they'd suspected. "Been hanging round the theatre again, darling? Seen Daddy?" Not on your life – I've been hanging around the set of *Bedroom Farce* hoping Chris'll come back from the bar.

No way they could see I just wanted to get out of their prison.

A scene. The Marquis family at breakfast. (Sociology essay: "Breakfast is the flashpoint of suburban family tension. Discuss.")

Robina (sixteen, beautiful, distracted) silently munches cornflakes.

Mother (Julia Marquis, to you) dashes in and out – "Cuttings from the *Gazette* about Job Opportunities – my god, those files, don't say I left them round at Jessica's, they're vital for today's meeting on the new Scheme for Unemployables."

Brian (twelve, knock-kneed and beginning to sprout acne) has the unshakable conviction that you're panting to hear the entire plot of last night's horror movie. "And Quatermass Queen, the one with the tentacle-arms and snakes in her hair, she starts strangling this monster, the fiery-eyed one that's just speared the Muscly Monk with his laser-beam fingertips…" Robina is distracted by the fact that she was never allowed to watch horror movies when she was Brian's age.

Father? Poor dear David Marquis, mid-nervous breakdown owing to last night's appalling Box Office receipts, has left at 8 a.m. Oh, he's an actor, is he?

Hope springs – maybe this is a suburban family with a difference? Hope tumbles. Director? No. Designer? No. Actually he's what they call an Administrator. My dad, an actor? He hasn't got the guts.

The boredom, the sheer yuk of it swept over me as I pushed my way out of the sick smell of the phone box. I was flaming hot and soaked with sweat.

The fresh air hit me. I took a huge gulp of it – I could've got drunk on it. I'm a drunk Robina, a free Robina, a girl who can stop being called bloody Robina – they even used to call me Banko in the third year: Robin, robbing banks, Banko! I can decide to call myself Mary or Kate or Abigail if I feel like it, I said to myself as I sauntered along (and up, and down, and round and round) the sunny streets of Bristol.

Why did I phone, then, if I was so free?

Be honest. I phoned because there's a cavern the size of Wookey Hole inside me. (Another of Mum's Improving Trips.) You're like putty when you're born. Your parents nag you and bribe you (they call it loving you) and bash you into some sort of shape that suits them. Then they stand it up and show it to the world. They say "That's her! That's Robina! Isn't she sweet?" And if you shout "No it's bloody not!" … what then?

But it's all you've got.

Canals here – well, sort of harbours: small boats, yachts with their sails furled, bright white cruisers with frilled curtains at their little windows, converted fishing smacks with fancy new names like Jasmine and old working names like *King o' the Catch*. A salt smell in the air, a breeze from the Atlantic. You could live in one of those boats – imagine! – get away from everyone, be utterly alone. I wouldn't miss anyone. Yes, I'd miss Cal.

Odd – I've never dreamt about Cal, even though we've been friends ever since we sat next to each other the first day I walked into that school. Cal's amazing, so calm. Everyone likes her, yet I'm the one who's her friend. I can't understand why Mum hates her. Cal gets on with her mum and dad, she loves going on holiday with them to the villa in Spain – she seems a goodie-goodie but she's not, she's great.

I didn't dream about Chris, not even when it was really hot. "Hot?" Cal once asked me. "Did you…" "No I did not," I said. I didn't ask her if she did, with anyone. She's Catholic, she wouldn't. Anyway, where would Chris and I get, to do it? In any case… OK, I was chasing him. He was hardly interested. Yes, he was! Sort of. Till he found out I was Dad's daughter.

Dad spoiling my life. Dad with blood on his hands. Dream… *I was in the bar at the theatre and everyone famous was there – Pauline from "EastEnders" and the Queen (she was dragging Princess Anne behind her in a pushchair) and Meryl Streep and Samantha Fox and Rowan Atkinson and Paul McCartney looking like Lady Macbeth – his hands were dripping with blood. But he was wearing a bikini, a pink bikini with big black spots all over it. And then he wasn't Paul McCartney, he was Dad, and he was shaking blood all over everywhere and laughing. And I was in the middle of all this, I was the engine of it all. It was a merry-go-round with me as the central pole. I was whirling it round and round – I was getting tireder and tireder and wondering how long I could go on…*

I was the engine of it all. Power: that's it, I want power over my life.

Where was I? I took out my street map and had a look. Hey, the SS *Great Britain* was just round the corner! Good work, Beano. I remembered it quite clearly now that I was walking towards it. It must have been about four years ago we'd come. October. Cold! I'd got so cold Bri called me Blue Bean. Now the sun made everything sparkle and (come on, admit it) the place did have its attractions. A cabin cruiser was chugging down the wide brown river towards that little harbour I'd seen, and over the other side the bank was so steep that the rows of terraced houses were leaning over each other to get a view. The pavements had been cobbled here to give it a quaint feel, and coach-loads of tourists were shuffling along with cameras dangling and guides chivvying.

I went to the very edge and walked along it like a tightrope. Maybe I should just lean over – fall in and drown? Scabby woman with my fiver, why haven't you jumped in and drowned? Why shouldn't I? Solve everything, that would.

But the water was mucky, floating with cigarette cartons and plastic mugs and rainbow streaks of oil. Not today: I'll steady myself and shift my bag on to my offside shoulder. I could hear the chattings of the current coach-load, and a call wafted over the water from the cruiser, "Tea up, Geoffrey!" and, irritably, "Not when we're docking, Mavis!"

Step – step – step along my tightrope.

There were feet coming along towards me. Feet in trainers like mine but tattier – falling apart, in fact. Who'd shift first? Or would we both walk on, collide, knock each other over the edge into the filthy water?

I could see the socks inside the trainers – they were Dayglo green, the sort that used to be in fashion years ago – and they kept walking towards me. Didn't change their pace one iota.

Well I wasn't going to change direction – why should I? If those trainers didn't want to end up in a splash they'd better get out of the way before I...

But it was me that skipped sideways on to the cobbles.

Stinker! It's people like that who get other people killed on the roads!

I turned round to see what sort of bastard it was. He was still walking along the edge – a tatty sort of boy/man (hard to tell). Thin enough for one of those refugee camps.

A recorded voice was booming out from behind the pay-booth where some Americans were pushing their jerky way through. "First really big ship... Famous engineer Isambard Kingdom Brunel" I remember that: what kind of a name is that for a human bean, Kingdom? "Launch ... many famous people ... momentous occasion ... severe weather..." Struck an iceberg, did she, like the *Titanic*?

I walked back a bit and found a shiny black bollard – capstan they call it, don't they, where they tie the ropes round. It said Society of Merchant BRISTOL Venturers. I put my bag on the cobbles, rubbed my aching shoulder and sat myself down. Well, I was a Venturer. Venturing where to? I didn't know just yet.

Seagulls overhead – hope they don't plop on me. More people. Same country accent: I tried practising it in my head, pretending I was a rosy-cheeked barmaid serving cider.

Come on, Bina, you're supposed to be Thinking. Should I get a job as a bar-maid? Change my name? Robina – I ask you! Marquis isn't that bad, but it's odd, identifiable.

So. What name? It's like going into films, or rock. No, it isn't – I don't want a name everyone'll remember, I want a name everyone'll forget.

Another coach-load crowded near me with their guide shouting at them in – what language? – was it German, maybe Dutch?

Suzanne, I could call myself Suzanne: it was the name of one of the actresses Dad had brought to stay at our house for a week because there were bedbugs at her lodgings. Suzanne … Brown. I'll scribble Robina Marquis off the front of my dream-books and put Suzanne Brown next to the Strictly Private.

I turned round for my bag and —

It was gone.

I turned back. "I'm going mad," I said to myself. "If I turn round again my bag'll still be there."

I paused, turned round again, and stared. It was gone. The spot where I'd put my stripy barrel-bag was empty.

I leapt to my feet. Panic. Where the hell?

I looked all round – saw that boy – that Dayglo sock bastard – he was running past the end of the cobbly bit by the café and round the corner – and he was carrying my purple stripy barrel-bag.

Chapter 4

Greased lightning wasn't in it. I was off after him like Zola Budd.

Round the corner – long street of offices, warehouses, parked lorries, vans. He was nowhere.

He could be anywhere, behind – underneath – one of these lorries.

I walked slowly round each vehicle, then peered underneath it, coming out and round and on to the next one. Peering along the road under all of them, searching for disappearing disintegrating trainers. All the time knowing that while I'm round the back of a lorry he's probably scarpered off up the road into limbo.

After five lorries and two vans I gave up. I ran to the T-junction on to the main road.

Right. Left. No sign. Nothing.

I stood – puffing – sweating – frantic. I'd got no money, no night things, no spare clothes, no bank card.

No dreams! The bastard's got my dreams! My paper for writing them on! Everything!

I stood there with my hands in my pockets, and cursed.

Hands in my pockets. In the left, the folded-up street map. Big deal, I can still find my way around this blasted place. In the right – jingle jingle. I'd put half a dozen 10p pieces in there to phone home, and I'd only used one.

So that's it, is it? Hell's teeth, I'm just going to

phone again, am I, only an hour after the last time –
"Little Bina's got herself into a mess, ran away from
home and got her bag nicked, can you come and fetch
her quick cos she's very frightened?"

Am I cobblers. Take a deep breath and think again.

He'd go to the centre of town, wouldn't he. He'd
want to spend some of my hard-saved eighty-five
pounds (less rail £7.50, £3.75 hair-cut, £5 for Scabby
Woman and B 'n' B £14 – plus bits of loose change)
before going home to Mum. Would he have a mum?
Not one that cared whether he nicked my bag or not.

What I had to do was go back to the town centre
and… And?

Wander around looking for a boy in half-dead
trainers with green Dayglo socks showing through.
Great.

Hang on, though. Cash card. If he'd got any sense
at all (which he probably didn't) he'd go to the bank
and try to draw out money. But he'd need the code
number as well. My diary was in my barrel-bag and it
had my cash card number in it, hidden amongst the
telephone numbers under RM Essential. Would he
find it?

Well, I'd find a branch of the bank where they had
a cash point in the wall, and I'd wait.

My feet were sore, I was roasted like Sunday pork,
and I didn't even have the money to leap on to one of
the buses that flashed past me. I passed a telephone
box – opened the door to see if it was vandalized or
smelt of sick or dog-muck – it was OK. Lifted the
receiver, listened to the dialling tone, put it down
again.

By the time I got to the city centre I was sweating

all over – I'd get to stink at this rate. And I'd got no clothes to change into! (I'd have to phone home. No I wouldn't.)

Wandered round trying to find the bank, my head full of curses.

Here's the bank – see the queue along the street from the cash point – people who've got pots of money in that bank and all they've got to do is press a few buttons and it'll spew out a wad of crisp notes into their delicately manicured hand.

I stood over the other side of the road from it and watched.

And watched. No Dayglo bastard.

Come on, time to move. I'm getting to hate the guts of every filthy rich person that hovers in front of the machine. Yesterday I was one of them, wasn't I?

What to do? Wander, what else. Stop thinking – thinking only makes you scared. Into Boots, try a few eye-shadows on the back of my hand. "Can I help you, madam?" No thank you, but it's nice to get used to my new image in your mirrors.

If I phone home and they come to get me, will they recognize me? It's like the story Mum used to read me when I was a kid about the white puppy-dog that got lost and its little girl owner looked everywhere for it and when she found it again she didn't recognize it because it'd got so dirty it wasn't her little white dog any longer.

I found an indoor market, full of crafty pots and some interesting earrings. I tried some on at £16.50 and thought – Dad's had a heart attack, Mum's on the verge of suicide. It could happen, if they cared that much.

41

I made a face at my face and it made a face back at me. They didn't care. As soon as I got back they'd start about Exams, Re-sits, Careers.

I looked at my face in the mirror. It started to swim. I wasn't going to cry, I was going to faint. I'd got nothing – no money, no dreams. I held on to the counter. If I fainted I'd be rushed to hospital in an ambulance and they'd summon Mum and Dad and as soon as I'd got better they'd start about Exams and Re-sits and Careers.

Swallow hard. My head begins to feel steadier. I've got no alternative.

I took off the earrings and went to find a phone box. There was a row of three, and the middle one was empty and even quite clean. They might not be in, Mum will've gone to the supermarket and Dad'll have gone back to work. If there's no reply it's a sign, it means I have to manage on my own.

Da-da, da—

I pressed in one of my precious 10ps.

"Hello?" Mum, breathless.

Can she hear me breathing?

"Hello? Robina? Darling?"

Yes, I'm the brick wall you're talking to.

"Darling…" She was pleading, she was down on her knees. "It doesn't matter about the results. Nothing matters, so long as you're all right. Nothing at all – just come back, and we'll…"

This dream: I had it the night after Mum-in-the-mud, the night after English Lit when I'd sat and stared at these dead simple questions – I mean, "Examine Mark Antony's Friends, Romans, Countrymen speech with a view to its effect on a modern audience". I dreamed. *I'm in this room, and it's totally dark. There's an audience of people sitting in the room in front of me, and they're singing, and they're in total darkness too. They're singing like Welsh people do, solid and warm and tear-jerking. But I'm separate from them. I'm up here on the ... no, it's not a stage, it's a swimming pool, and I'm walking along the top of it. It goes splish splosh, splish splosh, gently under my feet. I'm walking on water – I'm Jesus, I can walk on water!*

She was desperate for me to say something, but I wouldn't, I couldn't.

"Bina, I want to tell you something." This was a prepared speech.

I'm like a statue in this phone box. They should bring along a crane and pick the whole thing up with me in it and call it Frozen Communications and put it in some art gallery.

"Bina, it's all been very muddled lately. Life's not as simple as you think it is. You can't solve anything just by running away. You won't believe this, but I really do understand. Many's the time, truly darling, when I..."

I walk along the water, laughing. But then hands of steel get hold of my ankles and start pulling at me – pulling pulling pulling. I go on laughing – I resist them. But they're not steel now, they're snakes, and they're coiling round my ankles, still relentlessly pulling. I'm going under now.

"...job, you know, he has to fight every inch of the way, he gets so exhausted, so... I know you think Caroline's got the perfect parents, her mum not working and..."

43

I'm sinking into chocolate fudge cake. I'm going under – it's up to my armpits – it's up to my chin – my mouth is under – when my nostrils go under then I'm done for… Drowning again. Losing control. Fear of losing control. Losing everything, drowning in a sea of chocolate fudge.

"Maybe I haven't listened to you… Bina, darling, can you hear me? I'm sure we can sort things out if only – Damn!"

The pips were going. I could put in another coin, or I needn't. She's in my power, it's horrible – I don't want to hear any more.

I pressed in another coin.

"…seems to cut me off. Do you feel he cuts you off? Do you know, when you were little, darling, I used to think of you as the family barometer. Whenever I felt low, you'd go down with ear-ache or you'd trip over the back step and gash your knee. The pressure – it's been building up like a head of steam…"

I suddenly screeched at her, "I don't want to know!" and threw down the phone and pushed myself out of the door.

My dreams. I've lost them. I want them back. I'll walk round and round Bristol till I find that boy. I don't care about my clothes – I don't care about the money – I can steal some if I have to. I just want my dreams back.

I went back to the cash point in the wall. I went back to that blasted ship. I went on, and back, and I don't know where.

My feet got so hot and sweaty I took my trainers and socks off and walked along in my bare feet till I saw a traffic warden looking at me as if she'd get me arrested.

I went back to Temple Meads Station – the clock stared at me, nearly one o'clock, dinner-time – and went to the Ladies to have a wee and a drink of water.

Back along the river to get cool.

Way past the blasted ship, I turned a corner and saw this amazing soaring gorge above me. It had a bridge flying over it. Took out the map, found it must be the Clifton Suspension Bridge and the Avon Gorge.

Put the map in my pocket, sat on a wall for a bit, got my energy back. Craned my neck to look for a way up to the high high bridge, saw a rocky overgrown path over the other side of the road. Went across and started up it, had to stop every three minutes for puffs.

Didn't know where I was going or why. Yes I did know. I was going to wear myself out, then I really would faint and I'd get found by some kind little old lady who'd call an ambulance and… And then things would just happen. I wouldn't have to decide anything.

Climbing up, I forgot about Mum and Dad and the Dayglo boy and everything. I started working out how I'd have answered that Julius Caesar question. Easy peasy. I could have stood there on the hillside and quoted the whole of Mark Antony's speech in modern everyday English from beginning to end.

I got to the top and walked along a bit, and saw the suspension bridge flying away to my left. That'd be quite good to throw yourself off.

There was another little hill in front of me, with a kind of tower on top of it – observatory or something.

Dayglo was there. He was sitting on a bench near

the top of the hill, overlooking the throw-yourself-off bridge and the deep deep gorge.

Chapter 5

I walked up from his left and I could see where the canvas of his left trainer was coming away from its rubber base. His thin upper-arm came out like a stick from the wavy edge of his greyish-purple T-shirt: all skin and bone, no muscle at all. Not a sign of my barrel-bag.

I walked slowly towards his bench. He didn't look up – why should he? If I kicked him on the shin I bet he'd limp away and not even glance to see who'd done it.

I sat down. I left about three feet of bench between me and him.

The sun was hot. You could see he had two pairs of socks on, the Dayglo green ones with holes in and underneath some grey woolly ones, the kind that earnest ramblers wear. His mum probably got them from a jumble sale.

I said, "Where is it, then?" Staring straight ahead.

Nothing. I suppose he thought I was another weirdo like him that always sit on benches talking to themselves.

"It's purple, striped, shape of a barrel," I said. "I won't go to the police, I won't get you flung into prison. You can go to hell for all I care. But I want my bag back."

The foot twitched inside its gaping trainer.

"I'll tell you what was in it. Clothes. If you're that skint you can have them." That was flannel, but I'd say anything. "Cash card, rail card. No bloody good to anyone – unless you're expert at forging. Personal stereo and three tapes. But there's money. And one big fat envelope. I want them back – money, envelope. Now."

One foot crossed over the other. There was a toe-hole in the other trainer, too.

"I'm going to follow you round till I get them back. I can run fast. I'll follow you home. I'll sit on your door-step till you get a High Court injunction to throw me off. What?"

He'd said something.

"What did you say?"

"Tame. Pathetic. Boring."

What was he talking about? Me? My attack on him? My – my dreams?

He was mumbling again. "…as mine. Mine've got guts spewing – kidneys torn out – dragons munching legs 'n' arms – tigers tearing – devils screaming – orgies of —"

I was on my feet – I'd tear *his* kidneys out. "You've read them! They were private – you…"

"Shouldn't have left it lying around." Lying? It was right beside me! "Anyway…"

"Anyway?" My voice came out like a croak – I was choking with rage. He hadn't only stolen my dreams, he'd raped them. I wouldn't let anyone see them, not even Cal – they're part of me – I wouldn't show them around any more than I'd lie flat on my back while they slit me open and stared at my pulsating innards.

"Threw them. In a bin somewhere." His head had jerked up when I leapt to my feet – now it sank back on to his hollow chest.

I swallowed hard. "Threw them. In a bin

somewhere." Stood firm on the footpath. I'd got my voice back: "Well then. We'll go back to all the places you've been since you nicked my bag and we'll look in every single rubbish bin till we find them."

"'Ll've been emptied."

"Some bloody hope they will. If it's no go with the bins, we'll try the waste tips."

I'd thought he might suddenly take off and run, but he seemed glued to the bench. I sat down again – though I kept a hand ready to grab his jeans if he tried anything.

"Well? Shall we go?"

"You can."

"Thanks, but I'll wait for you."

We sat. Down below us the river was gleaming. A little twin-engined plane buzzed overhead, Brian'd know what kind. Wonder if this type's keen on engines?

When he said that about kidneys and tigers I'd felt a shock of fear. But now I thought, he's a worm, he's squashable. It'll be easy getting him to show me where he's chucked my dreams. He's a flea and I'm a spider. Watch my web.

"What for, anyway?"

"Oh! I'd forgotten you could speak. What did you say?"

"What d'you want them for. Write them down for." When he asked questions they came out like statements.

"That's my business."

"Not if you want me to help find."

"I'm studying psychoanalysis." He wouldn't understand.

"Crap."

"What?"

"Psycho stuff. Drive you crazy if you weren't already. Got a fag?"

"Fag?" The gear-change jerked me. "You shouldn't kill yourself."

"Why not. You Catholic or summat."

"No – why?" It was like being shot at by a sag-bag. "Anyway, it costs."

"What's money." Again, no question-mark – said like a final judgement.

"Money's all right if you can get it," I said.

"You can get it."

"Like you got mine?"

"Spent it."

"Spent! You can't have!"

"Did."

"Eighty-five pounds!"

"Wasn't."

"Sixty, then."

"Fifty-five pound seventeen pence."

I suppose that'd be right, with my bits of change. "Give it me."

"'N't got it. Spent it, like I said."

"On?"

"Things."

Great. I had the criminal, I had the confession. "OK. Police." And I leapt up and grabbed his arm.

He sat there. It was like holding the twig of a tree when there's no wind blowing.

"Come on. We're off to the police station."

A family came walking by – Mum and Dad with two kids, one licking an ice-cream and the other in a pushchair sucking an iced lolly, red sticky streaks running down its chin. The Mum and Dad looked at me and Dayglo as if to say, "Love! Not like it used to be in our young day." I felt a total loony standing there with his floppy arm in my grip.

But I couldn't let go of him, I had to get him to the cops. What I really wanted was to bash him to smithereens. Big deal: then it wouldn't be him helping the police with their inquiries, it'd be me.

I let go of his arm and sat down, right next to him this time. "I've told you. I'll follow you round till I get them back. Money and dreams."

Sudden thought – if I follow him to whatever rat-hole he lives in and he rapes me, in court they'll say "You did what, Miss Marquis? You followed him to his home?" But no. This one couldn't rape a prostitute if she came and sat on his knee.

Try a new tactic. Interrogators always come in pairs, Mr Nice and Mr Nasty. I'd tried Mr Nasty – zilch. Here comes Mr Nice.

"I'd buy you a packet of fags. Only I've no money." Silence. "They sell ice-creams up there. I could just do with one. I'd get you some fags at the same time. Only I can't."

"Don't smoke."

"I don't smoke, it's you that smokes."

"Don't."

"You don't? What did you ask me for a fag for, then?" He was a nutcase and no mistake.

Try again. "Where d'you live? Round here? I'm just visiting. Why d'you go to that blasted ship? Sent you out for some fresh air, did they – stop you watching endless videos? They're like that, aren't they? 'Make good use of your time, darling. I can't bear to see you lolling about in here when it's so glorious outside'."

Nothing. I knotted my fingers together to stop me grabbing him round the throat.

"They'll be furious about the money. I won't know what to tell them. If I found it – well, I'd be over the moon. I might go wild, do a dance, fling a ten pound note at the kind person who found it. Sorry? Did you say something?"

"Told you. Spent it."

"Show me." Was that a grunt? "What you bought with it? Camera? Ghetto-blaster? Whole Top Twenty on compact disc? Dinner at the Hilton?"

No grunt. Oh – drugs, I suppose. And yet… He didn't look like he was on drugs. He didn't smell like he was on drugs. Chris'd pointed out this addict that hung around the theatre café: he stank like mouldy meat and his skin was terrible, so spotty it was almost rotting away. This one was pale, pasty, underfed, but not rotting away.

"Anyway, I told you. I want my dreams. They're important to me. I'm trying to find the meaning of my life."

"Die."

"What?"

"You're gonna die. 'S meaning of life."

"Course you're going to die! Not right away, though. You've got time to do a few things first. Question is, what? And they don't help, do they? They just tell you. They never listen."

"Keep outa their way."

"Messed you about too, have they? They always

do. Did you get out from under? Find a place of your own? You haven't got a job, have you? Know where I can get one?"

Silence. He'd gone again, disappeared back inside his spindly self.

I suddenly felt all floppy, like Dayglo. I'd tell him how miserable I was and maybe he'd understand. "I read in this magazine about dreams. It said you're afraid of part of yourself, so you suppress it. It's the part of you that the world can't accept. But it's vital to you. It comes up in dreams, and you need it." I thought he'd say "Crap" but he didn't. Encouragement of a sort, that was. "Yours are gory, are they? Well, we all want to murder our parents, it's only natural. Or we're in love with them, ha ha. All that Oedipus stuff, it's ridiculous. You couldn't marry your mother, could you? I mean."

Imagine old Oedipus killing his father and marrying his mother. I'd seen the play – some touring company did it – they'd made it into SF, all in space, and Oedipus was a two-headed Zaphod Beeblebrox character trying to kiss his mother with one of his faces and weep sorrowful tears with the other.

I watched the cars stopping to pay their money at the toll-house and wondered if any of the drivers were tempted to put their foot down on the accelerator and go Zoom-Crash! down to the bottom of the gorge. I would, if I'd got a fast car and I'd lost my dreams. I could feel my heart going boom-ba-di-boom – imagined my heart when it was dead, all its auricles and ventricles shrinking and wrinkling like burst balloons after my head got bashed in on the rocks. What's the point of a head when it can't pass exams?

What's the point of a heart when it's lost its dreams?

He said, "Zoo."

"Zoo. Pardon?"

"Hate zoos, can't stand 'em, want to tear doors off cages 'n' let 'em all run out."

"Oh. Do you?" Was this mere chat, or relevant?

"He's seen real kangaroos, my dad. Great big hops, big as a whole cage up there," with a jerk of the head in the direction of (I supposed) a zoo. "They shoot 'em."

"What?"

"Say they're pests. Kangaroos! 'N Australia. They shoot 'em. An' here we shove 'em in cages an' chuck crisps at 'em."

"You're not supposed to. Feed them. What about my stuff? What's zoos got to do with it?"

"Don't you care then?" He suddenly turned on me. Full face, for the first time. He was wild. "Them stuck in there, all they can see is bars, an' us saying 'Look at them, aren't they sweet', and them with legs that can run a hundred miles and skin made for boiling heat standing there in cages in rain and snow and hail-storms and having babies that've never seen the bush and the jungle and the step —"

"What step?"

"Step–p–e! Plain! Prairie! You ignorant? Don't you care?" Then, in the tiniest second like the one he'd blown up in, he turned his flaming face away again. "Nobody cares."

What the hell was all this about? "You want to go then? To a zoo? They got one here, have they?" Would he really let rhinoceroses out of cages so they charged people in the suburbs and trampled them down and ate them alive?

Silence again. Had he finished? No. In the old monotone, "Up there. I went. Chucked yer stuff in a bin."

"Right. Let's go. How far is it?"

"Up there." Head-jerk again.

I stood up. "Well?" He stayed sitting. "You coming?"

Silence. But then he got up, and we went.

Chapter 6

He was that pathetic and undernourished I kept on having to stop and let him catch me up. I used to keep myself fit with swimming. Swimming! Imagine… Plunging into cool blue-green waters, coming up half way across, a smooth crawl to the other side and a fish-like turn, then smoothly, coolly, cleanly back again.

Despair: he had, he really had thrown the whole bag in a bin. Fight back: no he hadn't. How long since he'd nicked it? It'd've been a bit before eleven o'clock. What was it now? 14.47. No wonder my innards were craving for an ice-cream, a beefburger, a ham-and-salad sandwich, a hot-dog.

"Is it far?" I looked at him, and he was ever so slightly shaking his head. "What's your name? Mine's Robina." Oh, I was going to've been Suzanne Brown, years ago, before he stole my bag.

"What? What did you say?"

He went furious again, like over the animals. "I said Vern! V–E–R–N! Short for Vernon! You deaf?"

"You shouldn't mumble." This was going to be twenty years hard. Why couldn't I just have gone to the cops and reported my stuff missing? 'Cos I was missing myself, that's why. I felt a chill in the air all of a sudden.

I glanced sideways at him again. Vern short for Vernon. "You can't just've thrown it all in a bin!"

"'S too heavy. All that paper."

"They were my *dreams*!"

"What's in your head?"

"What d'you mean, what's in my head?"

"Dreams. Don't need 'em scribbled like that. Stay inside your head."

That was a speech, for him. I thought about it. "I know they should be. But they're not. They go. They're like a film you've seen – no, it's worse, they're not even inside your memory, they disappear, it's as though you never had them. You've got to write them down, all the books say so."

Hey – I'd still got my page of dream-interpretation, hadn't I? Folded up in my jeans' pocket? I felt. Only the map and a few 10ps. I remembered – I'd stuffed it back in the envelope with my dreams.

No dreams. No meaning.

Would he've had time to take it home in between stealing it and me finding him? If so, why didn't he stay at home, hiding?

Maybe he'd got some of my stuff in his pockets. I glanced. Yes, there were bulges – and you could see every bulge, he was that thin. Not big enough for a Walkman – lumpy bulges, not square.

"'S up here."

"What? Oh, the zoo. It costs money to get in, have you thought of that?"

"Doesn't."

"What?"

"See."

We'd get arrested. He'd try to sneak us into the zoo without paying and we'd get caught and taken down to the Police Station. Mum and Dad'd come, get interviewed by the Chief Inspector: "Do you think, Mr Marquis, that your daughter might have been

57

involved in something more serious – breaking and entering, drug trafficking?"

That chill in the air: there were black clouds moving over from the left. My Walkman! He can't have thrown away my Walkman! OK it had the batteries stuck in with sticky tape, but it kept me going through fifteen Agatha Christies and hundreds of hours of revision – well, pretend revision.

I thought, Don't know about a wild goose chase, this is a lame duck chase. Maybe it wasn't even him that took my bag – maybe it was one of those American tourists or someone I didn't even see, and Dayglo here – Vern – just happened to be running along the wharf. All that stuff about my dreams, he's invented it – he's insane, cuckoo.

In which case following him around is a waste of time. But what else is there to do? And I saw my bag in his hand. Didn't I? Or was that a dream?

I'd got my 10 pences, but if I stopped to use a phone box I'd lose him. There were trees along here, and the leaves rustled. I was shivering. I'd tied my jacket round my waist first thing in the morning: now I untied it and put it on. I'd sworn at my thick sweater when I packed my bag in the Laura Ashley room, but I'd be needing it soon. Where in hell's name was my sweater now?

We'd arrived at the zoo. He stopped a little way away, and so did I. He'd obviously got some plan. There was a white lodge with a man in a booth and a turnstile, and above it a notice saying Bristol Zoo and a row of black silhouetted animals in wrought iron walking along in a line. I could see what he meant: animals, with a life of their own that we can't understand, caught – imprisoned – like butterflies pinned on paper for us to say "How beautiful". But weren't zoos supposed to be for studying animals, and saving species from extinction?

He'd gone over to the hedge that ran along each side of the white lodge and he'd sat down. Well, I couldn't go in without him, so I'd have to do the same.

"What now, then?" No reply. "We going to storm the gates?" Nothing. So it's like that again, is it?

We sat there.

What'll they be doing at home now? Having an anxious late lunch, said my innards. I can just see them: Mum with a cottage cheese salad lying uneaten on her plate – Dad in the office amid piles of unread scripts, unable to concentrate for fear that his darling? hated? infuriating daughter lies at the bottom of the Thames, the Severn, the Atlantic...

I must have scared them. Yes, this'll sort them. Show them I'm not going to be messed around. If I go back I could...

No. I can't face it. They'd say "But what were you doing all that time, Bina? In your room, revising – all those hours in the exams – what were you doing?" Answer: freaking out. Keeping going. Freaking out underneath, keeping going on top.

I've got to stay here. With Vern. Vern who's pulling me round Bristol like a dog on a lead.

I could feel a lump in my throat like solid sick. It'll choke me. Vern's choking me with frustration. I'll choke him. But if I throttle him I'll be no further forward. I felt a warning in my head, like my Warning Dream. It said, Watch it, Beano, or you'll go over the edge. You'll go wild, like you did in the third year with Sharon Latimer. Remember, they had to drag you off her. I could see it now, like a slow motion film, Mr McNaughton peeling me off Sharon Latimer like peeling chewing gum away from a desktop... She deserved it, she'd been tormenting me for weeks, calling me Comic Stripper because I told better jokes than she did.

But it'd flashed up like neon in my head once or twice since then: Warning. If you get like that again, people'll back away, they'll stare at you like they did then ... petrified.

Terrified, terrifying. Like my Warning Dream. *A huge office, full of computer screens and flashing lights. And daleks whirring around and chanting in their piercing electronic voices, "Awful Warning! Awful Warning!" And I...*

I couldn't remember it! I'd lost it, lost all my memories, my dreams!

What would he do if I panicked? If I stood up there outside the zoo and started screaming? The zoo-man at the turnstile'd come rushing out and Vern'd get scared and drag me away to the place where he'd hidden my...

No, he'd scarper, and leave me to get hauled off to the nearest loony-bin.

I could remember some of it. *I was floating overhead – I wasn't visible to the daleks and I thought I should come down and see what the Awful Warning was. I flew down and looked at the computer screens to see what was written on them, and they all said in huge letters...*

I'd been dreaming, that's what I'd been doing. If I told them that, they'd think I meant daydreaming.

They wouldn't understand how earth-shaking it was that I'd been dreaming at last. Bina who never dreamed – Bina whose moods they all dismissed as "adolescence" – Bina who they'd trained not to let on what she really felt, who didn't even know what she did feel – that same Bina had a dream each night, and she wrote down every single word of it so that it would tell her how to be different, be real, really be.

And now they were gone, my dreams, my real me – gone, thanks to this worm, this Dayglo Vern, sitting (asleep, was he?) beside me.

Maybe I was actually crazy. That's what my dreams showed – that underneath my standard teenage exterior I was conkers, stark staring.

And the computer screens all screamed, "IT'S YOU!" I knew what they meant: they meant I had to look at myself. So I looked down at my feet. And I saw that they were the feet of a fish-scaled claw-toed monster. Then I looked at the rest of myself, and all the rest of me was a... Oh god. I was. A monster.

We were still sitting there. I can't be loony if I can remember my dream, surely? Dreams are always weird. *But then a god-like creature appeared, and I protested to him – her? – that if I was a monster, then monsters were GOOD creatures – I was good, truly I was – if only someone would kiss me like in fairytales.* No, no – I've made that bit up! Maybe I've made the whole dream up! I'm making everything up – failing my exams, Vern stealing my bag – everything!

I blinked. Shook myself. How long had I gone off into my dream, my panic? A second or ten minutes?

I heard a rustle. Vern was taking something out of his pocket. I turned and looked at him.

It was my packet of dried fruit, half eaten. He was untwisting the top of the bag so that he could eat some more.

Chapter 7

"Here," he said (or some such generous word). I grabbed the bag from him and got my fingers round some dried fruit and stuffed it into my mouth. Sticky, sweet, luscious. I gave it back to him and he took some, then he gave it back to me. And so on. It was all gone in about one minute fifty seconds. Then he screwed up the bag and threw it about two feet away. Should I rave on at him for being a litter lout? I just sat there staring at the bag as it unscrewed itself and the wind took it and blew it up into the air and away.

"What did you do with the cheese?" I asked him casually. "It was going smelly – runny."

"Leaked all over the pages."

"What – over my dreams?"

"Don't know. No – over the clean stuff. Chucked it away."

In a bin. In the zoo, or somewhere. I got furious again. "I don't believe you! About the money. Sixty quid!"

"Don't believe, then."

"Go and get it, so as we can get into that zoo."

Boring old silence again.

"Go on! It's starting to rain!"

A drip had landed on my head. Since we'd sat down it had gone from bright and shining to slaty grey and gusty, like a set for *Wuthering Heights*. People had been wandering past us and paying the man in the booth in the white lodge and I'd been envying them opening their purses and their wallets and shelling out all that money. Now there were people putting hoods or sweaters or newspapers over their heads and running for the entrance.

I stood up and said, "C'mon, we'll get drenched out here."

But he sat and didn't look up and said, "Hang on for a coach."

"Hang on for a… Why?"

Silence. Then, "Here's one."

A coach was stopping – it had German writing along the side, and it was one of those elegant ones with smoked glass that have loos and videos and champagne brought in ice-buckets like on Concorde. Its engine stopped, the door slid open and a courier-woman in high heels came down the steps and put up an umbrella. Then all the rest of the coach-load started piling out and running for shelter. When about half of them were out, Vern said, "Right. Now. Run."

"You mean…?"

He was halfway to the white lodge. I got up and ran after him.

It was that easy I wish I'd thought of it myself. We huddled with the Germans, and I kept my jacket hood over my head and we waited till the courier had pushed her way through. The man in the booth did something to the turnstile, then we all pushed in. The man might have seen us, Vern and me – he was trying to do a rough count, I could see his lips – but there were some screaming kids trying to push in behind the Germans and he had to go and sort them out.

I was inside the zoo, and I hadn't paid. I'd never done anything like it before. Well, it was his fault, it was him stealing my money, he made me do it, Officer, I'm not guilty, M'Lud.

The German crowd put up black umbrellas and grouped themselves round the courier. Vern wandered casually away to the right. He didn't seem to mind getting wet. What could I do? I followed him.

I love zoos. I go into them and make faces at all the animals and ask them what they think of us daft humans standing there staring at them. They're probably doing a Social Survey. Camels are my favourite, they're so disdainful, and…

Vern had put his hands over his ears. He was still walking, quite fast now, and there was a shrieking, a sort of "hoop! hoop! hoop!" coming from some swinging things, some kind of ape, in cages on our right. He started to run. He ran to the shelter of a pavilion place and so did I.

"You're neurotic," I said. "They're only expressing themselves."

"Like babies. You'd say babies are 'only crying'." He still had his hands over his ears, and he was shouting. "Gibbons – they're gibbons, crying. I don't want to hear 'em."

"Well, you are hearing them – you're hearing me. Take your hands off your stupid ears and think what we're going to do next. All the stuff in the bins'll be soaking wet."

We sat there. I could see a bin from where I was sitting: it was made of wooden slats with a red-painted metal bin inside. There was stuff piled up in it till it'd spilled over on to the pathway. What a jolly afternoon we were going to have, nosing round people's dripping wet yuk. If you could call it afternoon when there'd been no lunch.

The rain was starting to slacken. "Come on," I said. "I'm not staying here all day."

I wandered out of the shelter towards the bin. Would he follow? Orpheus in the Underworld, I shouldn't look back. I looked back. He was drifting along, looking half asleep, hands still over his ears.

I stopped at the bin. "Go on. This is your job."

"'S your stuff." But after a minute he let his hands drop and picked at the rubbish in the bin. All small stuff.

On to the next one. "Why d'you come if you hate the noise they make? Where's your father if he's seen real kangaroos? Don't believe he has, anyway."

His head came up from the bin, and his eyes looked like little flames of candle. His voice came out very quietly, like a teacher who's very angry and absolutely in control. He said, "'As your dad been in the Merchant Navy?"

Baffled, I was, and a bit scared. "No – why?"

"Well mine 'as. He's been everywhere. So shut it." And he went back to the bin.

In between bins he stood for eternities looking at the elephants. They were Asian ones – I could tell that from the label, but he said that Asians had one more (or was it one less?) toe than the Indian ones and different ears. "Look," he said. "Tusks sawn off." I was waiting for him to say they were drugged to keep them quiet – their huge eyes blinked as if they were half asleep. And eyelashes! I've never looked at an elephant's eyelashes before. One of them reached over the moat to wrench hunks out of the hedge: I jumped backwards when the great muddy wrinkled trunk came swinging over, but Vern didn't, he just went on standing there, staring. I thought he was going to stroke it.

We must have spent two or three hours in the zoo. Then we started on the town.

Have you any notion what people put in dustbins? I hadn't till then. Toilet rolls, new, unused. Toilet roll, used, in small smelly brown-streaked sheets – both the hard kind and the soft kind. All sizes of used... I won't go on, you can imagine. Half-finished knitting dragged off its needles and wrapped in its knitting pattern. Computer print-outs so big and heavy they'd wrenched the bin off its lamp-post. A contact lens holder – I recognized it, Mum wears them – still with the lenses in them. A dustpan full of horse manure with the dustpan's brush stuck firmly into the stuff. Five frilly nightdresses straight from mail-order, their labels still attached – I'd've nicked a couple only I didn't know what disease they might be carrying. Four identical high-heeled left shoes.

I might have got worn out, the number of miles we walked and bins we excavated, only he sat on every bench we came across and stared into space. I commented on the weather, "Brightening up! I'm steaming, aren't you?" till that got boring, then tried "Lads who wear after-shave are crap, aren't they?" or "Why do Americans all wear plastic raincoats?"

But what did I get out of him? Sweet Frances Adams, that's what. I couldn't find out anything about him, not even where he lived, though I told him my entire address (17 Daffodil Cottages, Bourton-on-the-Water) and my age (nineteen) and that my parents were in Saudi Arabia where my father was computerising oil production.

He was a demon wonder at finding food, I'll say that for Vern. Apart from what he found in bins – sweets, unopened crisp packets, seven corned beef sandwiches hygienically wrapped in foil – he went into a Chinese takeaway in a slummy area and asked for "Fried rice leavings" and we got a massive pile each, full of scraps of prawn and mushroom and sweet-'n'-sour pork. The people seemed friendly to him as if he often went there. The girls looked at me knowingly while the boss went behind for the stuff, and when they said, "Ten pence, please" they turned to me. I handed over a coin: that meant I'd only got two left, but it was the fattest and quickest-gobbled 10p I've ever spent.

I got furious with him about three times. "You must know where you put the stuff! You've got to remember – there's a brain in your head, isn't there – or maybe there isn't, it's filled with filth like all these dustbins."

But it made no difference. The angrier I got, the less he said. He seemed as happy as Larry trailing round the greasy dustbins of Bristol till nuclear war broke out or the police nabbed him for pilfering a used Tesco bag.

By the time my watch said 20.30 I'd stopped being angry – I was terrified. Not of going mad or facing home – just of simple things like sleeping rough and starving. "I'll have to be getting home," I said. "Or I'll miss the last bus. Only I've got no money for the fare."

He quickened his pace. I caught up with him. "You haven't spent it, I know you haven't. I want it. Give it me." He still kept just in front of me. "Give it me!

What if I get stuck in this place? Where'll I spend the night?"

He mumbled something.

"What?" I caught him up at last.

"Plenty of places."

"What kind of places?"

"Sleep."

So. He's one of those. He hasn't got a mum, he hasn't got a home to go to. He sleeps under hedges, in disused warehouses. He's probably got a private cache of cheap cider or meths hidden somewhere under a paving slab to help him nod off at nights, and a pile of newspaper to keep him warm.

"Well, your tastes may be more specialized but I like a bed to sleep in. They don't come cheap in a place like this. Unless you're thinking of a police cell, I believe they're free."

"Find somewhere. When it's dark."

"What?" But I'd heard him.

He meant he'd find somewhere to doss down, and that included me. Unless I took off and lost my only chance to get my dreams back.

There was an ache in my middle as if a rock was lodged in the place where all my habits had been – my going-to-bed routine of always brushing my teeth last thing of all so that my mouth felt glowing fresh before I curled up under my duvet and drifted off into sleep. And I've got no make-up remover – my make-up's inches thick – it'll go streaky in the night – if my eyes water, the mascara'll run down my cheeks – and I'll have no mirror to check my face before anyone sees me in the morning.

Vern doesn't care what he looks like. Mind you, he

doesn't smell – he must have got somewhere he can go for a bath at least once a week. And his clothes aren't any grubbier than some folks' at school, so?

We were somewhere near the centre of town. The shops had shut and people were wandering around arm in arm and going into pubs and restaurants. Pubs and restaurants! The fried rice leavings seemed a year and a half ago.

Vern made for a bench in a concrete space with trees and shrubs scattered around in pots, and sat down. I went and sat down about three feet away from him. It was as if I'd only just found him, except that now I'd start to wail like a baby if someone so much as knocked my little finger.

"Think tonight it'll be a boat."

"A boat." I sniffed. "Not the Hilton or the Holiday Inn? Oh I am disappointed."

"When it's dark."

"That'll be ages. Any suggestions? Fancy a film or something?" Nothing. "Well, I'm going to wander round the place, see if there's anything on. That new Madonna film sounds good. Don't suppose you read the reviews."

Silence. I'll get up and go. Not look back this time. And if he doesn't follow me, I'll still go.

I got up, and went, and he didn't follow me. I crossed the road and walked casually along a few streets, and for a while I thought he'd probably be following at a distance. I'd almost got the feeling he was attached to me, or maybe I was attached to him. Maybe he thought that since there'd been sixty-odd quid in my bag there'd be more on my person, and he only had to wait till I nodded off and then he'd nick it

70

and away.

But he wasn't coming. I glanced behind me. No one. After a bit I stood and stared. He didn't come.

There were three or four cinemas round here – I stood and gazed at the pictures outside and thought, "Space, cowboys and sex. That's the world on celluloid – space, cowboys and sex." That seemed pretty profound, till I found another cinema where it was all violence, sex-and-violence, and violence.

They probably needed actresses for that sort of thing – to work in sex-and-violence films. I mean, it wasn't the kind of work RADA trained you for. I don't suppose you really got hurt? But where would you go to offer yourself? There'd be a seedy little office somewhere with a phone number given only to those in the know.

The YWCA. If I could find it I could sleep there. In the morning when they wanted the money I'd say "I've just got to phone home," and get Mum to promise to pay, and they'd have to wait till she turned up. Where was it? I should ask.

I looked round. I walked on and tried looking people in the eye. Surely someone would look at me back – recognize me as some kind of fellow human being? It's starting to get dark – a small bright star twinkles cheekily at me from between the chimneys. I'm coming up a hill near some kind of huge church or cathedral - there must've been a service or a concert going on because people are pouring out – one of them's singing a high trill and her boyfriend's cross: "Please, Miranda! Wait till we get home!"

No one casts me a single glance. I turn round, and it hits me between the eyes. Bina, I say to myself – you think these people will be nice to you because you're your parents' daughter, because you're Cal's friend and she's pretty, because you're Chris's... Well – they won't. You're just you, you're on your own and you've got nowhere to sleep, and nobody cares.

I walked down the hill again towards the cinemas and the shops, towards Temple Meads Station. In that case there's no need to worry. You may as well sleep under a hedge or in a doorway, and get arrested for being a vagrant, and get put in jail where you'll be treated like muck but at any rate it'll be warm and you'll be made to have a bath. They told us that in Soc. Ed: when you're put in jail you're made to have a bath.

I never realized before how much I love baths. Hot water. Soap. Shampoo. A towel that I've put over the radiator to get warm so I can wrap it cosily round myself and hug myself dry.

I was crying.

I was coming near to the place where I'd left Vern sitting on the bench. Knowing him, he might be still there. I blew my nose. Pull yourself together, Bean.

He was still there. I sat down beside him – well, my standard three feet away. I had to blow my nose again, but then I said, "Getting chilly, isn't it?" It wasn't – it was a warm, calm, clear, beautiful evening.

After only a minute or so he got up and said, without looking at me, "All right. You coming then."

"Lead on, Macduff," I said. He probably didn't even know who Macduff was.

Chapter 8

I woke up like someone had kicked me. A dream! Where am I? I'm rocking – *I'm sinking, being pulled under by steel hands – I'm drowning…*

My terror-dream. I should have sat up, eyes staring and sweat pouring off my forehead like in some old Hammer Brothers movie.

But I just lay there, rigid, as if some wizard was standing over me with his arm raised holding a black wand and declaiming, Robina Marquis, you are turned to marble. You shall be as marble until… Until?

Steel hands. Drowning. Water – water… The gentle slosh-slosh-slosh of the river lapping against the sides of the boat had put drowning into my head.

But it wasn't my standard terror-dream. I grope down inside my mind for it … I need my dream, I've got to have it – like I had to have that fairy-and-goblin curtain material when I was about six and I thought I'd die when Mum said No, we must have the blue flowery material because it would outlast my six-year-old fairy-and-goblin phase.

First: *A farmyard.* Farmyard – with cows and pigs and ducks on a…? *Pond full of elephants.* Elephants – of course, the zoo. *The elephants weren't swimming in the pond, they were floating on their backs, and one of them was balancing me gently on the flat tops of its upturned feet. I fitted them neatly, I was comfy. But then the feet began to stretch wider and wider apart, and I knew that when the feet were as far apart as I was long, I'd fall through to the heaving belly beneath.*

The belly was covered in long piercing spikes, and I was going to fall on them any minute, and thousands of spikes would plunge into me – puncture me, penetrate my flesh – and out would pour my life's blood, red and sticky, all down my body and down the elephant's body and streakily into the waters of the pond.

I fell. But the spikes didn't hurt me. The elephant's belly heaved up and down rhythmically and slow, and I floated up and down with it, and I could hear its great heart-beat like the heart-beat of a new and gentler world.

But I'd woken rigid with terror. Why? I shouldn't ask. I should leave it alone. That's what your dreams taught you – that some things were vile and threatening and should be left in Dreamland where they belonged.

And the heart-beat grew louder and louder and closer to my ear, and I heard the deep booming sound of the sea at its very deepest depths, where monsters live in total darkness and corpses of drowned sailors lie in coral dust. I hear the ghosts of the sailors laughing triumphantly because I've come to join them. I'm a mermaid they've captured, I'm their prey. Now one of them seizes me, and it isn't a man, it's an octopus with claws – it holds me in its tentacles, its talons dig into my flesh and my blood drips out through the holes in my flesh and my blood isn't red human blood, it's black like tar, like drops of liquid evil...

Rigid with terror – no wonder. I had to find pen and paper and write it down. I always did after a terror-dream.

It was still dark, middle-of-the-nightish, but I'd scribble something – I had to put it in my possession, take away the terror of it, put it under my control.

No pen. No paper. No dreams. They'd gone.

I was fully awake now. I was in this bunk, in this boat, this little cabin cruiser that belonged to God-knows-who, and the bastard who'd stolen my dreams was in the other bunk, just along there.

What could I do? Go to sleep again.

Impossible. Adrenalin was pumping round me. I had to lie in the darkness, still as a corpse. And I had to do something, too.

I knew what I should do: I'd whisper to myself.

When I was scared in the middle of the night at home, I'd lie and comfort myself by talking in whispers to Somebody. I pictured this Somebody as a kindly woman sitting on the other side of a roaring log fire knitting a thick brown woollen sweater and listening to me with rapt attention. I could whisper now. OK, Vern was in the other bunk in the prow – the bows? But...

There was a bit of light, now my eyes had adjusted to it, from distant street-lamps I suppose. Was Vern awake too? I turned as far as I could without rocking or creaking, but I couldn't see him. Would his eyes be open or shut? Knowing him, he'd keep them shut even if he was awake, just to get me confused.

The boat rocked gently of its own accord. I whispered, "What time is it?" God knows. Terror terror terror – I hate hate hate dreams – no I don't, I hate hate hate not being able to write them down. Where are my written-down dreams? In the council tip with everyone's old baked-bean tins, that's where my dreams are.

"Go to sleep. Sleep sleep sleep. Wake up feeling fine – new day, lots to do, jump out of bed...

"What's today? Day Two of New Free Robina. Sorry, 'Suzanne'. Oh, drop that, I can't be Suzanne, never was Suzanne, never will be.

"Day Two – assuming it's tomorrow. Where am I? In a stolen boat. Not stolen, we haven't moved it an inch. Commandeered, that's the word. Easy – just lean your shoulder against the plywood door, give a sharp bash, and crash! goes the bolt. Worst part was swinging out over the water – the only way to get into this Fort Knox of a Marina – clutching the slithery pole – trying not to shout 'Help!' – leg splayed out over the harbour all murky and oily below... The Boat Club must know only lunatics'd risk it.

"Rigid – now I'm shaking from my dream. Quivering inside. I never used to dream. I only started to dream when... My first dream I can ever remember was on the first day of exams.

"I tell a lie, I did dream when I was little. I woke up a few times and got Mum out of bed all bleary-eyed and irritable in her nightie telling her a bogey-man was after me. First she was terrified there was a burglar, then when she'd searched the house from top to bottom she got mad and shoved me back to bed. You can picture it, can't you.

"After that, nothing. People used to tell their dreams, lurid ones, sexy ones, when we were crammed into the locker-rooms during wet breaks. All about running for trains they couldn't catch or being sat on by scaly monsters, and they got hold of books that told you that it meant Sex. It always meant

Sex. I used to listen and wish I'd got something to offer. I was on the outside looking in. I even thought of making some up. They belonged to a club I wasn't qualified to join, they were at a party and I hadn't been asked."

Was that the echo of my whisper wafting around in the darkness? "A party and I hadn't been asked … hadn't been asked." It went into harmony with the lap-lap-lap of the water. The water was close, I could almost have been lying in it. The water felt gentle and friendly. My terror had gone. The cushions I was lying on were plastic-covered, but they were adorably comfortable since all I'd expected was a paving slab. It was the kind of bed that made into a table and bench-seats during the day and you just took the table off its legs and fitted it into some slots for night-time. It was a double bed – a bit squashed for two, but cosy. Imagine the boat-owners cuddled up here, planning their trip up the Severn and along the canals, whispering "Don't wake the children!" – who'd be asleep where Vern was now.

I knew my whispering'd comfort me, and it did. I closed my eyes and conjured up my whispering vision: the great log fire, the rocking chairs, Somebody knitting and listening, me talking. The rocking of the boat's like the rocking of our two chairs. I can see the candles on the mantlepiece, I can hear the tick-tock tick-tock of the clock in this comfort-house of my mind.

"Remember me confessing to Cal that I never had dreams? She said it was because I was super-normal. I said 'It's not me that's super-normal, it's you.' I wonder if she really is? Life's so simple for her.

Boring but simple. Mum with the tea ready – she even makes Cal's sandwiches for a school trip. I asked Cal if it didn't make her feel like a baby. No, she said, she was allowed to go to discos and watch videos, so who cared? They were stupid about boyfriends, but... Then she asked me if I fancied Terry Baines. Terry Baines!

"Spain. Hot romantic Spain – the villa... Her mum says we'd be welcome to rent it for a couple of weeks. Why can't we? It'd be great. But no – Mum and Dad can't find time to get off work together. 'It wouldn't be worth dragging all the way to Spain just for the three of us, darling.'

"I'll have to go back. Home. I'll hitch-hike. This bloody boy won't cough up anything. You listening, Vern? I wouldn't trust you further than I could throw you – though that'd be a fair way, you're flimsy enough.

"When it's light I'll get up quietly and slip out of the boat. Good thing I slept in my clothes.

"Slip out? Some hope. He'd be awake in a flash.

"I'll just say, 'I'm off. See you.' He won't bother, I've got no hold on him. It's the hold he's got on me that's the trouble. Why did he trail round all those dustbins? Waste of his time. He's got plenty of time to waste. He seems to know about dreams. He has dreams like I have dreams. Maybe he's curious about mine – that's why he's keeping them."

We'd found cornflakes in a plastic container in the cupboard. There was no milk to go with them, but we had water to drink – a luxury boat, water comes out of taps! – and some Rich Tea biscuits from a tin. Vern said it looked like the owners were coming to use the boat again soon: we'd better clear off quick before it was light in the morning, specially as it'd be Saturday. I asked how we were going to wake up because I for one didn't have an alarm clock on me, and he said, "Always wake up when I want. Just have to think about it."

Then he'd got some blankets out of the chests under the bunks at the end of the boat, turned off the torch he'd found in another cupboard, stretched himself out and gone to sleep. Just like that. I had to fumble for the torch in the dark and work out for myself how to fix my bunk. Then I got to work with some hard green soap I'd found beside the sink, washed my make-up off as best I could, examined my face by the light of the torch in the little mirror hanging there, then tucked myself in.

Now I'd stopped whispering, the boat was hollow and frightening again. Splosh – splosh – splosh – there was water all round me. Maybe the boat leaks – we'll sink, and no one knows we're here so they won't even send out a search party….

Whisper again. "Home. I'll creep home. Shut my ears while they're going on at me, run upstairs, lock my bedroom door. There's no key, there never are any keys to the rooms of these posh new houses. My favourite house was in Leicester. 'Poky little rooms,' Mum said. They weren't poky, they were cosy, crammed with our toys. My dressing-up box – I used to dress up long after everyone else had grown out of it – Mum got embarrassed, as if I was retarded. I'd put on a frilly pink dress and dance to next door's rock music – they had it on super-loud, the walls shook. That was before we could afford a 'better house', before Mum got a job, before we moved to Exeter. That only lasted a year and a half. Then Posh Living where we are now – Dad got a pay rise and Mum got promotion. You there, Vern? Fascinating, isn't it.

"Posh Living. I won't go back. I'll stay here and get a job in a café at one pound fifty an hour. I'm brilliant, I'll be manageress in a couple of years. You don't need exams, you only need personality. It's all about Cash Flow and Customers per Square Metre. I'll do business studies at night school.

"Phone Chris. Chris. Went away. Didn't phone. Moved on. His last kiss… Embarrassed. Hate him hate him hate him. He *used* me. What's 'used'? He's got his career to think of. So have I! Big deal: My Career.

"GCSE. You took it. You failed it. You're brilliant, so you say – but you failed. You sat there, Robin Banko, and you wrote such total rubbish they couldn't give you an A, B or C for a single subject. Not, Robina darling, a single bloody subject. Now, tell us, darling, simply and clearly – tell us what you sat there and wrote. In your exams.

"I can't remember."

"Can't *remember*? I tell you, I'm not giving you a penny more for clothes, I'm not paying for any driving lessons when you're seventeen, I'm not shelling out for another disco, I'm not giving you another lift to a party that everyone else in your year's going to and you'd be a freak if you missed it. Dad goes on like that, especially when his secretary's off with a nervous breakdown again. If he'd give me time I might find a proper answer. But they never give you time. They never listen.

"Remember. Exams. I sat there. It seems I did write something. No one said I sat there and wrote nothing. I didn't read any of it over afterwards. Yes I did – when English Lit was over I read my last sentence before she collected the papers, and it said, 'Julius Caesar is a filthy no-good rubbishy play because it doesn't have enough women in it. But politics is like that, isn't it.' At the time it seemed it was a fabulously intelligent thing to say."

Close my eyes, try to remember ... try to remember. Maths – I do remember the Maths exam – it was near the end, I was at screaming point. I remember thinking all numbers look the same, none of them mean anything on their own, but when you string them together they have a sort of magic to them, they're an incantation like witches sing when they circle round the cauldron cackling. Five, seven, two- ... xy— bracket-five- ... cd-plus-eight- ... ab-bracket ... cackle cackle cackle ... five, seven ...

"Up the Plata channel – a bugger that one is..." I woke up.

No dream. I fell asleep.... cackle cackle – I dropped off. How much later is it? The boat's still rocking, the splosh is still sploshing, we're still afloat and —

Vern's talking. "Unloading – it was the trip when Jack Flint got his thumb crushed under the..."

I was wide awake. He's talking. I'll find out something about him.

"Lizard, size of a ruddy banana it was, down at me feet there. I put me 'and down, an' it slithered up on to it and up me arm as far as me shoulder. An' there it stayed, starin' at me with those great lizard eyes, from start o' loadin' to t' finish of it. I thought of bringin' it back 'ome with me, but it couldn't have stood t' trip, four weeks on me shoulder back to 'Ampton Roads, an' me not able to dress nor undress neither."

He must be dreaming too. What the hell was he talking about? And his accent – I hadn't noticed his accent before.

He wasn't saying any more. I wanted to tell him, Go on, say something sensible. Tell me about Mr Vern and Mrs Vern and all the other little Verns.

He started again. I held my breath.

"Turtles. Japan, that was. Into Osaka an' up, couple of days we 'ad, Arthur an' Jim an' me, all mad about turtles. Ever seen a turtle layin' eggs, lad? Agony. Eyes poppin' out, breath stopped – never seen owt like it. Agony."

Where's he got all that from? Some kind of Gerald Durrell character, is he, going round the world collecting creepy-crawlies? Does he know I'm listening? Should I turn over and start snoring?

I closed my eyes. Opened them again.

"Whales. Did for 'em, the buggers, they did for 'em, bloody Australians. Bastards. Lyin' there, gaspin', eyes terrified. Blood all over t' deck. Dream about 'em I do. Blood all over t' deck, drippin' over t' side. Sea's red wi' it."

I could hear his breath – it was puffy and fast. He was mad with those Australians. I said, before I had time to think about it, "Dream?"

Not a second's pause and he'd answered me. "Dream. 'S a mountain. Me hanging, on a rope. Water coming down, pouring all over me. 'S warm." The accent's different. Back to Vern's voice. The other must be his dad. "'S not water, 's blood. 'S all over me.

Mountain – mountain tips forwards. I'm hanging off it. Rope's not rope, 's elastic, 's getting longer and longer, I'm going down, an' down, an' down – I'm looking down – an' 's a whirlpool – steaming…" His puffy breaths got even faster. "'S boiling, bubbling – I'm getting nearer and nearer – heat's coming up from it – I'm boiling, sweating, cooking…"

"It's only a dream," I said.

"Only a dream. Wake up, Vern – it's only a dream. I won't let 'em get to you. Get talkin' to it, Vern. Tell 'em to go away. Tell me all about it. Let's get to what it means." His dad again.

"What does it mean, Vern?"

"Mean? Means I've to be strong. Tell 'em they can't get hold of me. 'I'm off now, you're not gettin' me,' I've to say. 'It won't 'appen, your dream can't 'appen if you tell it to go away. Except if it's warnin' you.'"

"Warning you?"

"Tellin' you summat you need to know. I know, I know. 'But you hide, Vern. Not got to hide'."

"What d'you mean, hide?"

"Hide. No hiding. No place to hide."

"What from?"

Silence. His breaths got steadier, quieter. Then they got softer.

Go on, Vern – tell me about knowing, and hiding. "Tell me, Vern?" But no. His breathing was deeper now, very rhythmic. He was asleep. Unless he'd been asleep all the time?

I'll keep awake, see if he starts again. Listen to the slosh-slosh-slosh, feel the rocking motion floating through me as if I'm part of it – close my eyes – I'm on my rocking chair and I'm...

Awake. I'd fallen asleep, and now I was awake.

Opened my eyes. There were curtains dangling above my head, and under the frill I could see it was starting to get light.

I'd have to say something. It came out in a hoarse whisper, "It's morning, nearly."

He sat up, and so did I. We looked at one another like two cats glaring at each other before a fight.

He looked away and lifted up a curtain. Said nothing, got out from under the blanket. Folded up the blanket, lifted the bench under his mattress, put the blanket underneath. Smoothed it out so it wasn't wrinkled.

"Neat, aren't you?" I said, still in a hoarse whisper.

"Don't leave tracks," he whispered. "Only sense."

I heaved myself out, folded my own blanket, lifted the boards and sorted everything till it looked how it'd looked last night. Sat down, lifted another curtain: there was a pale dawn out there, a star or two still: it'd be hot again. Soft light beginning to shimmer on the still water. It would be great along the river, up the estuary. "Can't we take it out to sea?"

"They don't leave petrol in it, stupid."

"Cornflakes." I got the bowl from last night – imagine, I hadn't washed it up! – and poured myself some. "Want some?"

"Don't eat mornings."

"Nor do I, I only eat cornflakes."

He didn't laugh. "Move, we've no time."

I gobbled them down – there was a whole day ahead of me and no guarantee of food – and washed them down with water. Rinsed the bowl under the tap, shook it and put it away. "Thanks, Mr and Mrs Don't-Know-Who. That was great."

We went to the door. Vern had jammed it shut last night. Now he just wrenched it open.

I said, "Don't leave tracks?"

You couldn't expect him to be logical, I should've learnt that by now. He jumped off the boat.

Not a soul about. I peered at my watch: 05.47.

I swung round the high fence pole after Vern with a lump of excitement in my throat: we're going to make it, we'll outwit all these boat-owners, property-owners, we've had a free night and we're going to get away with it! Oily waters down below me streaked with rainbow. This time it didn't occur to me to be frightened. "Wow! T'rific!"

He turned round fiercely. "Sssssh!"

"Where are we going?"

He half walked, half ran on without a word. I was in his thrall: I followed after.

Chapter 9

Early morning's not my best time, specially when I've spent half the night dreaming terrible dreams and the other half listening to some loon droning on about turtles in Japan – but it was great dawdling along by the river. The air was all fresh on my face, I could be a loon myself, fling my arms about, shout across the mud-flats (they looked just like the muddy backside of yesterday's elephants) and listen to my shout dissolving in the air before it reached the other side.

No one was about. Not even a rowing boat on the river. A few birds with long beaks were poking around by the water: how come they stay so clean when they're always delving in the mud?

A huge lorry lumbered by. Then nothing. I ran into the road, did a Highland fling and ran back on to the pavement. Vern wandered slowly in front taking not a blind bit of notice of me, not even when I shouted at the long-beaked birds and made them flap up into the air crying like out-of-tune seagulls.

Where were we going? I didn't care. Don't think about money. Don't think about home. Don't think about anything.

A police car shot past. Coming for me? Will it screech to a halt, go into whining reverse, fling open the door, and shout, "Robina Marquis, I presume?" No, it disappeared round the corner at fifty miles an hour, off to a dawn raid on drug smugglers.

I knew where we were now – we were back at the Avon Gorge. There was the wall I'd sat on! A little way along, Vern stopped and sat on the very same wall and gazed up the gorge, like I'd done, at the high flying bridge. No, you couldn't throw yourself off, folks must have done it too often, they'd put massive fencing all along the sides. I sat down beside him.

"I had this dream last night," I said, conversationally. "Did you have any dreams? Mine was ghastly. All about... I was terrified, it was all about... I can't remember it. I never can remember my dreams if I don't write them down. But some bastard went and stole my pens and paper."

He got up and wandered back the way we'd come. I'm not following you any more, I thought. Then I turned back to see which direction he was going, and he'd disappeared. The whole wide road in front and – he wasn't there. He can't have vanished? There's a road just opposite – he must've gone up there.

I ran, turned up the side road. He was there, ahead of me, sauntering. God, I am stupid. How long's this going to go on? I'm exhausted. I hardly slept last night.

It was steep here, and my legs ached. A milk-float was groaning its way up and a boy of about my age ran to and fro with a milk-crate. I kept well behind Vern. I wasn't going to show him I wouldn't let him out of my sight.

Up at the top there was a right turn, but he went on. Hey, I recognized this bit – it was near the top of the rocky path I'd come up before! If we follow this top road along a bit we'll see the toll-booth for the suspension bridge and...

There was a bench just here. He sat on it. So did I, to get my breath back and rest my legs.

"You were dreaming, too," I said after a bit. "You were gabbling on. D'you remember? I wish I could remember that dream of mine. I told you, I never do. Mind you, there's one dream I have regularly, I don't need to write it down because I have it so often." Dreams, I'll catch him in the net of my dreams. "I'm in this vast black cave. I know it's a cave, even though it's so dark I can't see a thing, 'cos there are voices calling all round me and they echo. The echo goes on and on and round and round – the cave must be hundreds of feet high. I know that if my feet leave the floor of the cave then I'll float upwards and my head'll hit the ceiling and my skull'll get bashed in and I'll die. So I try and cling to the floor of the cave with my bare toes, but I can't because it's all smooth and there's nothing to cling to, and sooner or later I'll start floating upwards and then I'll bash my head in and get killed. And all the time the voices are calling and echoing…"

I wish he'd say something. I wish he'd ask me, "What are the voices saying?"

"They're saying to me, 'Do it! Do it! Do it!' You can imagine, it sounds like a million owls in that cave. Then it happens. My feet leave the ground, and I start to float upwards. I'm floating up – and up – and up – I don't know how far the roof is, I don't know when my head will crash against the rock and my brains'll get bashed in and I'll be dead."

Vern got up and ran, straight down the steep hill into the undergrowth.

Well, that's it. That really is it. I'm not going after him. I'm going to phone home and reverse the charges and get them to come and fetch me. No I'm not: first

I'm going to wander round Bristol and try and get myself a job, then I'm going to persuade the manager to give me an advance of a few pounds so I can get myself something to eat and find somewhere to stay. Maybe the manager'll be kind, he'll say, "In some kind of trouble, are you? But you're a good kid really – you can come and stay with me and the wife, if you don't mind babies that is… Oh, you'll baby-sit? Great, we'll give you one pound an hour."

There was a rustling from the long grass down the hill – yes, it was the path I came up yesterday (was it only yesterday – or a million years ago?) and Vern reappeared out of the undergrowth. He'd got a piece of paper in his hand.

He came over, shoved the piece of paper into my hand, and vanished down the same hole.

"Hey!" I half got up, then I looked at the hole he'd gone down and at the paper in my hand.

It'd got my writing on it. I read it. *"– as if it was their natural habitat. There were sea-horses (always my favourite) and Dad said kindly, "Would you like…"*

My dreams! My *dreams*!

Down that path. I was off.

Zig – zag – zig – zag. No sign. I stopped, puffed – you puff as much going down steep hills as you do going up, and your thighs hurt.

A noise in the jungle to my left. I plunged through the brambles and the cow parsley and long grass towards it…

He was sitting underneath a high bit of cliff with my purple stripy barrel-bag beside him and a sheaf of my dreams in his hands.

Blind with rage: I know why they say blind – I couldn't see him, I couldn't see anything – I didn't think what to say, I was just saying it, shouting it, fury pouring out of me like hot tar – my hands were on my hips and clinging on so as to stop myself tearing his straggly hair out, gouging his eyes out, strangling him till his voice went gurgle-croak and his body went limp.

"You had them all the time – you trailed me round – you bloody filthy lying bastard – you poked my head into every shit-bin in Bristol – you led me up hill and down dale till my feet were dropping off – you made me steal some people's boat – I could've been got by the police – I might be festering in jail now - hand-cuffed – criminal – you don't care, you're criminal anyway - I wouldn't be surprised if you'd murdered half a dozen innocent people and cut them up and kept their pieces stashed away in the hole where you've been hiding my bag and my things and my money and my dreams…"

Stopped. Panted. Then abruptly I was looking at him, seeing him, because he'd put my dreams back on top of the bag and he'd got his head stuck down on his knees and his shoulders were shaking.

Is he crying? Is he a baby really, a stupid kid who hides your toys because he wants you to get mad and spend lots of time trying to find them because otherwise nobody'll take any notice of him?

No, he wasn't, because his head came up and he threw himself back on the ground behind him and he was rolling around in a heap of laughter. Laughter!

It was ridiculous – it was crazy – but I couldn't help myself. I flipped from fury straight into hilarity and

90

collapsed on the ground beside him, rolling around in helpless laughter too. The ground was lumpy and bumpy and there was a thistle somewhere that I kept rolling over on to, but I didn't care, I was helpless, and so was he.

Eventually we calmed down. I lay there, looking up through the jungly grass to the sky. Not a single cloud. It was incredibly quiet, with distant traffic noise making it seem even quieter. There was a bird in the trees a little way off, making a loud tick-tick-tick noise – I suppose it was warning its mates there were some hysterical humanoids hereabouts. I could hear Vern puffing, then breathing deeply, then breathing more steadily. My god, he's raving bonkers and so am I.

I didn't know what to say, whether to say anything, whether to grab my stuff and run or lie here all day and go to sleep.

I said, "What I told you before – you were dreaming, you must've been dreaming, you know. You were gabbling on about lizards and turtles and Australia and whales. I thought it was kangaroos you were so het up about?"

"'Stralia's got a coast, you know. All round. They get whales, kill 'em, only there's hardly any left cos they killed that many."

"And turtles – Jim and somebody else, as wild about turtles as you were, and them laying eggs or something. How d'you know all that? You can't've been there? Or was it dreaming?"

"My dad."

Yes. "Him that was in the Merchant Navy."

"He went. Saw everything."

"Collected things, did he? Animals?"

"*No!*" He sat up like a shot and his face was right over mine, blazing. "Are you thick as a post? He *loves* 'em. They *live* there. He watches 'em, leaves 'em there. Where they belong." His face disappeared and he lay down again.

I wasn't going to answer him back, even with "He wanted to bring that lizard back – was he going to keep it for a pet?" – not if he was going to be like that.

"Anyway," he said. Anyway what? "You can say things to your dreams."

Ah, this was what he was on about last night. "Say what?"

"You in that cave. All those echoes saying 'Do it Do it'. You say to them, 'Do what?'"

"I can't! I'm asleep!"

"Think of the dream when you're awake. Get the kind of feeling - feel frightened like you're in the cave. Then when you hear the voices, you say 'Do what?'"

I thought about it. Well, maybe I could. But not now. "Who told you that? Your dad? Where's your dad? Where d'you live?"

Long silence. That's it, I thought, he won't say any more. Then suddenly, "I'm going to see him. Want to come?" It sounded like a real question.

"Come where?"

Nothing.

The bird had stopped tick-ticking and was trilling away cheerfully. I suddenly thought – My dreams! My clothes! My Walkman! My money! I've got them back!

I sat up and leant over him and grabbed my bag. The dreams were all in a mess on the top, so I got hold of them and put them underneath me to stop them blowing away (not that there was any wind) and hunted through the rest. Walkman – complete with head-phones. Underclothes. Cash card. Necessities – I didn't think he'd have sold those. At the bottom: my purse. I opened it. Counted it. Fifty pounds in notes – one two three four pound coins – two 20ps and three 2-pences.

"You spent seventy-one pence of mine. You can bloody well treat me to a couple of Cokes when the shops open."

He said, "Do what? Anyone knows what they're saying."

"What're you talking about?

"Dreams, stupid."

"Dreams? Yours tell you what to do, do they? Go and see your dad, ask this girl to come with you? They're telling me to go on the stage and act, but I can't do it, it's the one thing Mum and Dad are dead set against." Funny, that. I just said it as if I'd known it all along. I did – I wanted to act. I WANT TO ACT!

"… tell you, just like that – sometimes don't. 'S the day for seeing my dad. He's in hospital."

"Oh, poor thing. What's wrong? Had an operation or something?"

"No."

"Aren't you hungry? It's ridiculous not eating any breakfast. I want some hot buttered toast and strawberry jam like they have on farmhouse holidays in Enid Blyton."

"Enid who?"

"Blyton! Enig Blighter, like John Lennon said! Don't say it – 'who's John Lennon' – I can't stand it.

Winnie the Pooh, heard of Winnie the Pooh? Mrs Tiggywinkle? I suppose you spent your childhood going round the world in a cargo-boat."

I thought he'd hit me. He didn't.

I'd better see what I looked like. My mirror. Yes, there it was stuck at the bottom of the bag in a corner. And my comb! This was civilization.

Well, I didn't look too bad. A bit washed out, and I wasn't sure if this hair-style was entirely Me, but it was a change. Give Mum and Dad a shock. That's what I meant it for.

I'd felt a bit sticky and dirty first thing but it'd worn off now. Do you get used to being filthy and smelly – do you stop minding that people back off you 'cos you stink?

He'd got up, and he was looking at me as if to say Coming? supposing he was the kind of normal person who said that kind of thing. "Hang on," I said. "Got to get my bag packed neatly, haven't I? Everything fitted in before people started messing about with it."

Then we were off down the hill. Chatting, almost.

"Where do you live? Or are you on the streets?" Hell, that was the wrong phrase – or maybe he *was* on the streets? Sold his body to that kind of man for lots of money? "Where d'you get clean, wash your clothes?"

"There's places. Launderettes. Swimming baths."

"So you live rough?"

"House got taken. When they took my dad to hospital."

"They can't do that! Where's he going to go when he's better? I mean, they can't just take your house away!"

"Can. Take you to court, court takes it away."

"And you, where are you supposed to go? How old are you?"

"Sixteen."

"And you've just got to wander the streets?"

"They'd find me somewhere. But I'm not having them shoving their noses in. My dad'll come out. We'll get somewhere."

"But isn't there anyone – haven't you got an aunt or a friend or…"

We were down at the main road.

"Where are we going for breakfast? You've to stand me those Cokes, remember."

"'S you's got the money."

"I bet you've got some. Where did you hide all this? What else've you got there?" I wished I'd had a poke round when we were up by the cliff – he probably had a little cave in there behind the brambles.

But he was off again. From behind he looked like a giraffe, spindly but purposeful. What would he do in the autumn – winter?

I caught him up and tried a few more questions, but he'd cut off communications.

When we hit the city centre, cafés were open, people were everywhere, cars jammed the roads. Aren't people stupid? They should all get up at five in the morning, then they'd see what the world looked like without them. Though – I suppose they wouldn't.

We went to a café and I told him to get what he wanted. I didn't look at his tray till we reached the cash-out, and wow! he'd bought the lot: bowl of cornflakes with sixteen packets of sugar, sausage, bacon, egg, tomato and chips, three bread rolls and a pile of butter and jam. "Both trays together," I said, and the girl said "Eight pound ninety," and I had to stop myself falling over.

But I was mellow. I'd got my toast and strawberry jam, I'd treated myself to a doughnut as well, and I'd got my bag and my money and my dreams back. I looked at him across the table like you look at a pet dog that's enjoying the Nourishing Marrowbone Jelly you've just given it.

"Haven't told you anything about me, have I? Well I'd better, 'cos today –" in between massive mouthfuls of toast – "I've got to make up my tiny mind what I'm going to do. I thought I could make it on my own here, but I'm not so certain now. I'll have to go back some day. I thought that out last night. They'll find me, or I'll need something from them. But I can't face what they'll say. How can I get them to shut their mouths – leave me alone – stop them saying 'Come and see the doctor, darling'?"

He went on scoffing food.

"I flunked my exams, see."

He was rivetted by that news. One piece of sausage slid down his throat and another went in his mouth, no pause.

"Fs, Gs, and the Big U. OK, that may not be great earthquakes for you, but people like my folks press you. Nag you, urge you, bribe you. You're nothing but an exam machine to them." Whole slice of bacon disappeared. "Boyfriends – they're 'wasting your time, darling'. I had a great thing going with… Well, he was Front of House at the theatre. Managed the audience and the ice-creams, ignoramus. It was love. It was for me, anyway. I'll never forget the day he left.

A Sunday. He'd said he 'might phone me'. Ever waited sixteen hours for someone to phone? Every hour's got sixty minutes in it."

Galloping godfathers – he wasn't listening to me so I started listening to myself. What a whinger! Here's him – no parents, no roof over his head, on the streets, sleeping God knows where – and here's me moaning on about waiting sixteen hours for my boy-friend to ring and being terrified that Mummy and Daddy'll tell me off when I get back to the Nest. What am I going to do?

"I could go to Cal's. No, I can't, she's at the villa. I could hang on here till she comes back. Her folks'd take me in. I could phone the parents from there, use the Frys as buffer – Mum and Dad couldn't be rude to me in front of them. And if they started on at me, I'd just threaten to run off again."

He was into the cornflakes now, raining sugar on them like a snowstorm.

"Mind you, Cal will've phoned from the villa to find out her results. D'you think they'll've told her I've gone? Mum would, Dad wouldn't. Have you got a mum?"

For some reason I waited for the answer to that one. None came.

"No? What happened to her? Died? Drowned in the Bay of Biscay?"

He flamed up. I suppose that's what I wanted. "Gone! Can't you mind your own business?"

"No, I can't. People fascinate me. You, for instance. Why d'you get so mad if anyone asks you—"

"Shut it."

"OK, I'll shut it. And you can give me those

cornflakes. I paid for them, and I'm hungry." I reached over for his bowl.

Now I've done it – I'll have a fight on my hands and we'll get chucked out of the café and be arrested for Causing an Affray. But no. His hands dropped down to his sides, his head hung down like he'd suddenly dropped asleep.

"Don't be a moron," I said, pushing them back. "I don't want your soggy cornflakes. I just wanted to get you going. Look, there's a phone box over there, I'm going to make a phone call."

Chapter 10

I left my doughnut to show I was coming back. Though whether he minded or not I'd no idea. He'd probably eat the doughnut.

Something had decided me. I was going to phone, and I was going to talk. I couldn't plan my words. I just had to put in my ten pence, dial without thinking and see what happened. I'd tell them... I wouldn't tell them anything. What day was it? Saturday. Someone was sure to be home.

Miracle: a phone box empty. Miracle number 2: it's not vandalized.

How many seconds does it take to press the numbers for a phone call? It was while I was pressing our home phone number that I remembered. It flashed up in my head – no, it seized hold of my guts – the memory of that moment in the third year when I started hating them. They'd been OK till then – well, I hadn't thought about it, they were just my parents, you don't complain, you don't know any different – but then...

How could I have forgotten? It wasn't forgotten. It was put away in a dark basement because it was too horrible.

Now it surged up. Filled my guts like burning coffee. The picture of it: Mum and me sitting on hard grey chairs in that clinic, me being soft-soaped by this pseud doctor, Mum being probed about my Problem. And all the time I could read the writing upside-down on his desk: "Reason for Referral: Bouts of uncontrollable aggression." Bouts! As if I had them every day – I'd had *one*! And that was the day after (heart going bang-the-big-bass-drum 'cos I knew what they'd say) I tried to get a word in edgeways when they finally fixed my GCSE options. And Dad said, "Of course, for your creative subject – Art." And I knew that was it. No Drama. It was them I should have turned on, not Sharon Latimer!

Bang-bang-bang goes my big bass heart while I press the last number. Bang-bang-bang went my head, sitting on the hard grey chair.

I'd promised myself then and there: I wasn't going for a second appointment. He was a thief, was Dr Pseud – he was stealing my self-respect. I'd be marked for life – One of Those. So I promised I'd never hit anyone again if I needn't go back to Dr Pseud, and they said yes.

Ring-ring. An answer. They'd been waiting. "Hello?"

"Mum…"

"Bina! Darling! Where are you? Can I ring you back?"

Cunning – she could find out where I was from the town code. What the hell? I told her the number straight off. "I'll use this ten pence worth, then phone me." I could hear her breath go, as if she knew this was the beginning of the end.

"Darling – tell me what you've been doing. Tell me anything you want."

"I've been all right. I'd got some money." (I met this boy, he's living on the streets, we stole a boat.)

"I know. But how are you feeling? Do you – are you depressed or anything?"

That's it. Come-to-the-doctor stuff. "I'm fine, Mum." Very strong. "I needed some time on my own."

"Don't worry about the exams, darling, we'll sort something out. It's at times like this you start to see things in perspective."

"No, *I'll* sort something out, Mum. It's up to me, not you."

"Oh – " I could almost hear her hiccup – "it's so good, darling, hearing you talking like that."

The machine started to flash. "My 10p's run out."

"OK, I'll phone you, darling – wait there, I'll phone you back straight aw —" Cut. Yesterday's me would have gone outside the phone box and stood listening to it ring. But I stayed there, mind a total blank. Then just as the phone started to ring, I thought: I said it. I told her I'll do my own thing, I'm not letting them do it for me. And I sounded – balanced. That was the word they used as a condition: "So long as you stay *balanced*, darling."

Pick up the phone. "Hello?"

"Darling! You sound – fine. You wouldn't believe how good it is... We couldn't think what was happening to you."

"You're not to worry, Mum. I'm managing."

"That's great, great. And Cal's come back, she's longing to see you." She called her Cal – usually it was Caroline, disapproving.

"Cal? But they were staying on another week..."

"I know, but she phoned for her results – she was surprised to get me, she seemed to have hoped you'd be waiting by the phone – and when I told them you'd gone, her mother took the phone and was in quite a tizz and had a word with Mr Fry and then said they'd get the next plane home. They'd pretty well packed their bags anyway, she said, it's been raining there every day."

"Poor old Cal." I'd have a better tan than her at this rate, all the outdoor living I was doing.

"Mrs Fry was alarmed at you going. I'll ring her when I've stopped talking to you, she'll be so relieved. Oh darling, so am I. Relieved, I mean. The thing is..." Heart sinks. The thing is what? "You can't think what it's been like. Daddy's in such a state." They really care, do they – care what happens to me? Maybe one of Dad's visiting directors has seen me hanging around – spotted my talent. "You know Harry?" I knew Harry – pompous oaf, actor, so full of himself you wonder he can get any food in, comes to see us when he's "resting". "He's had a heart attack. Dad's oldest friend – he may not make it."

"Oh dear, I am sorry."

"No no, you won't break your heart, I know... But your father's taken it dreadfully. He won't go upstairs two at a time." Two at a time? "He won't mow the lawn, we've got to get an electric one. His job is so stressful, he says he'll have to find something else, except there *is* nothing else."

"Poor old bugger."

"What, darling? Try and imagine what it's like. First you. Then Harry. Then we got Brian back –" Brian! – "because I couldn't stand your father worrying that he'd fall down a rock face." They'd got Bri home! It was panic all right. But not about me. About them. "Come home, darling. We need you, truly we do. We love you. It's ghastly, you being

102

somewhere – nowhere – with all this…"

I put down the phone slowly. She was still talking.

I walked back over to the café. Vern actually looked up from his last bite of bread roll as I came back in. The doughnut was where I'd left it.

"I spoke to her. She was very pleased to hear me. My dad's friend's had a heart attack so he thinks he's going to have one too. Brian came home because Daddy couldn't stand the thought of him hanging off a cliff. Brian's my little brother, did I tell you? Have you got any, or sisters? They wanted him home so they could feel safe. They want me home so they can feel safe. They don't want any anxiety. No stress for Mr Marquis, please. Be a good girl."

I put half my doughnut in my mouth in one gulp, mulched it and swallowed it down. "Mind you, Cal's back from the villa. She cares. Though it was pissing with rain in Spain. Ironic, isn't it – sun blazing down on the streets of Bristol."

"What's a villa?"

"Holiday home. You can rent a week or a fortnight in one, or buy a share in one, but Cal's family have bought theirs for themselves. They let friends have it cheap. Dad's friend was going there next week. Well, he's got a fortnight in intensive care instead."

I felt sick. If I go home they'll want me to prop them up by being sweetness and light. So, I'll stay here and do something, get a job. What if there aren't any jobs? What if they only pay a pound an hour, are only part-time, I only get twenty pounds a week? The rent'll be twenty-five and then what about food? I could get two part-time jobs – forty pounds a week – you can't live on forty pounds a week… What about the Social

Security? They'll only phone Mum and Dad and get them to come and take me back.

I looked at Vern. He was staring into space. "You going to the hospital, then?" I remembered: he'd actually volunteered, invited me to come with him.

"'S afternoon. Two till four."

"Where is it?"

"Bus ride. Way out."

"That's stupid. How do they expect people to visit?"

"Don't."

"Was he really in the Merchant Navy?"

"Liar, am I?"

"What was his job?"

"Engineer."

"Did he have an accident? Break his back? Burn himself?" Head down on his chest again – I wouldn't get an answer to that one.

"How long's he been in hospital?"

"Ages."

"What happens to you, then? Where do you live in winter?"

"Places." He got up. I thought he was wandering off, but he went up to the counter and asked for a coffee. Then he took some money out of his pocket and paid for it. Money. He'd got some of his own.

Funny, I wasn't mad at him any more. I was amazed. I wanted to laugh. When he came and sat down I said, "You owe me. Go and get me a Coke and a bar of chocolate. While you're at it, get a couple, and some sandwiches for later. I'll have ham and tomato."

Chapter 11

He took me round all the places he'd slept in. Derelict cars parked in back alleys with their windscreens bashed in – you can climb in through the front and then over to the back, it's dry and quite clean and the fuzz never think to look. Station cafés like the one at Temple Meads – I saw the freckly man with the ginger hair, stared him straight in the eye but he didn't recognize me – you can't sleep there at night, Vern said, but you can buy a coffee during the day and sit there nodding off and they think you're just tired from travelling. Any café'll do, but you can't use any of them more than once in a while or they start chucking you out. Then you can wander round all night and...

"And what?"

"'S great. See the stars. Think about the sea."

"You ever been to sea? Or just heard about it from your dad?"

"Went on a trip."

"What kind of trip?"

"With kids. From a place I was."

"Place?" I knew that look: it meant Stop Asking. Had he been in children's homes? Youth Custody places? "But you never went on a sea-going ship, to faraway lands?" Silence.

Shabby streets scattered with litter, full of houses where they'd give you a bed and a bowl of cereal for a fiver, no questions asked. But where did he get the fivers? No use even putting the question. Anyway, I knew he was pretty good at nicking.

There was the Youth Hostel if you were desperate, he said, but they wondered where your back-pack was and you had to say you'd put it in the Left Luggage at the station.

"Don't you need a card? Membership card?" I'd asked if he was an expert forger, and I wouldn't put it past him. "You must have some things – toothbrush, change of clothes. You've got a special hidey-hole, haven't you, up there on the cliff-side? Where are we now?"

It was the Bus Station. I hoped there was somewhere to sit down, it was nearly half-past eleven and I was worn out and hot and sticky with all this wandering. But no, there weren't any cafés here, only kiosks to buy drinks and snacks, and you had to prop yourself up somewhere to nosh them. I suppose that'd be to stop folks like Vern – like me and Vern – using them to doss down in. Why shouldn't tramps sleep in cafés? They don't do anyone any harm.

"Are we going, then? To see your dad?"

No reply. I looked round – no Vern. Where the hell was he?

I walked round the corner. He was sitting propped up against the side of the snack kiosk, head on his chest, eyes shut.

Well then. Am I going to some strange hospital with him to see his dad, or am I going to wander around Bristol all day waiting to be picked up by the police or my poor darling anxious parents? Decisions decisions decisions – I've never made any decisions on my own before, I've just gone along with what everyone said. OK I refused to go to Gran's funeral last year, stayed at home and listened to the Top Forty top volume while I shouted out Nora's big speech from *The Doll's House* – "I was simply your little songbird, your doll…" Dad hated old Gran anyway, we hadn't seen her for years and she always sent me Californian Poppy Bath Salts for Christmas. I kid you not: each year rain or shine, Californian Poppy. You could smell it from the far side of the room through its Father Christmas wrapping paper.

I was standing there staring at Vern. He's a tramp – maybe I'm a tramp too. He looks like a waif. Do I look like a waif?

I rushed off with my barrel-bag to the Ladies. Turned on a tap: hot water! There were a few people around, but I didn't care, I stripped down to my bra and filled the basin and gave myself a real good wash. Then I took my bag into a loo and took everything off and changed into clean clothes. Back to the basins to give my hair a brush-through: I liked myself spiky, hedgehog, but I wanted a well-brushed hedgehog. I put on a bit of make-up – not like before, not like a freak, just enough to make me feel respectable. I'm not a tramp, I'm not having anyone thinking I'm a tramp.

I put on some gold dangly earrings I'd found in the bottom of my bag and came out feeling a new woman. I went and sat down beside Vern, who was still asleep, took out my dreams and started to sort them out.

They were all out of order. On top was the Queen with Princess Anne in a pushchair and Paul McCartney as Dad, and here was one I had near the beginning about being *in a space-ship – Brian and me were weightless and floating around, and what we had to do was to get some stability by getting hold of this firework, a sort of Catherine wheel that was going round and round and showering sparks in our faces, so we closed our eyes and a fire-fanged beast roared flames at us and burned a hole in the space-ship and I fell, still with my eyes tight shut, out into the bottomless black void.*

Here's my funeral. *There I was. But it was another me. I was sitting upright in a pine coffin high on a marble pedestal* – Yes, it was the one I'd dreamt the night before I got my results. Last Wednesday, before I woke up on Thursday. Two days ago. Unbelievable.

And my Comfort Dream. *Stretched out my whole body into the petals so that every square millimetre of my skin was softly touched.*

Reading my dreams felt like a cool breeze blowing through my brain. I was comforted and stimulated at the same time. It was like watching a film or a play and you're totally caught up in what's going on and you're taken out of yourself and everything suddenly has colour and meaning and magic and you forget that outside the rain's tippling down and tomorrow's homework hasn't been done and you've got to wash the car to pay Dad back for the money you borrowed to come to the film because you were skint till the end of next week. I was in my own world, my wild crazy chosen world – I was my wild crazy chosen me.

There was only a bit of spare paper left and some of it had got streaks of cheese-grease on, so I went over to the newsagent's stall and bought an exercise book for 35p. I'd write down last night's dream, and then I'd write down that recurring one, the one about the cave with the echoing voices.

While I was writing, I remembered what Vern – or

was it his dad? – had said about speaking to your dream. *"I'm sure I'm going to leave the ground and float up and hit my head on the ceiling, and all the time the voices are calling 'DO IT DO IT DO IT...'"* Maybe I could speak to it – say, "Do what?"

I had no problem feeling the feeling that the dream always gave me. I only had to write DO IT and... I can hear them, the voices, I can feel the terror of flying up at fifty miles an hour and crashing my skull against that hard rock – CRASH! – and my brains all spilling out in pieces and spraying round like sparks after a firework has exploded and floating down to the floor of the cave below... I'm trembling with terror.

I looked up to make sure I was still in the land of waking people, sane people, the everyday world of ham-and-tomato sandwiches... Yes: here was the Bus Station, and there was Vern sitting beside me with my ham-and-tomato sandwich in his pocket. I suppose he's alive? His chest was moving very gently up and down.

I stare at the page again. DO IT DO IT DO IT. My heart's thudding. I say, inside my head, Do what?

No reply. It was as bad as Vern.

He shifted. "Time is it?"

"One twenty-seven."

He got up as if he hadn't slept a wink. "Bus is one twenty-nine. Over there."

He set off towards the buses. I shoved my dreams back into the bag – no time to zip it up – and went after him. He got on a bus and handed some money to the driver and said something I couldn't hear, then disappeared upstairs. I fumbled in my bag and said "Same please," got my ticket, went up after him, and the bus jerked and started to move.

I sat down. "What's the name of the place? What am I going to do? Come in with you? D'you need your hand held or something?"

Then I tumbled to it. *That's* why his dad's been in hospital for such ages. *That's* why the hospital's so far out of town. He's in one of those Victorian institutions that were built out in the countryside so the inmates wouldn't contaminate decent citizens. His father's been put away for as long as need be till he comes to his senses: he's actually nuts.

I didn't dare look at Vern. Did his dad go mad with all the loneliness on the high seas? But you've got all the other men for company. Maybe he needed women, and his wife had left him, the bitch. Maybe she couldn't stand the loneliness without him. Or maybe she just couldn't stand him. Maybe he drank – sailors usually drink. Maybe he beat her up. Maybe he caught some virus from a jungle or a desert somewhere, and it infected his brain and slowly ate it away and he got hallucinations and tremblings and gnashings of teeth till eventually he fell into a coma and was flown home.

I tried to look at the scenery. Boring suburbs. Parks. Up and down, up and down. At my eye level, street-lamps. TV aerials: one of the drama groups did a sketch about James Logie Baird who invented the television, and the man who lodged in the room next door to him kept on seeing pictures flashing on his wall and they dragged him off to the lunatic asylum 'cos they thought he was seeing things, hallucinating.

"Big hospital, is it?"

"Big."

"What kind of ward is it? Surgical? I warn you, I

110

can't stand seeing people lying in beds with bottles hanging up beside them and tubes coming in and out of their noses. I faint. They won't want another patient on their hands."

"Dressed."

"What?"

"He's dressed. Walking about like you and me."

"What's he in there for, then?" I turned and looked at him.

He looked the other way, staring at TV aerials as if he was doing a project on them. Then he said, "They won't let him out."

"Why not? Will he bleed to death?"

He turned on me. I was getting used to that now. There was no one else on the top of the bus, so I wasn't even embarrassed. "He's got nowhere to go, has he!"

But the look in his eyes had a peculiar effect on me. I turned and looked out of the window again. I was suddenly scared – not scared of him, scared of me. I'd suddenly started to feel, not sorry for him but – feel for him. Feel what he must be feeling. Ghastly about his dad being in there – the only person Vern's got in the whole wide world, and he's shut up in there and not allowed to come out.

I felt it and I didn't want to feel it – I wanted to think about going home and facing what I'd got to face. I've got no time for him, he's fouling up my thinking space.

"He'd better go to the zoo and live with the animals. He'd be happy there."

He didn't turn on me. He said, "He's tried," and turned away. End of conversation.

I asked for my ham-and-tomato sandwich. It came

out squashed. I offered him half: no.

I'd just finished it when it was time to get off. I couldn't see any hospital near: it must be quite a way to walk.

Vern started talking. I couldn't hear what he was saying at first, then I got bits of it.

"Lying on this white bed, and they start taking my legs off. They don't have to saw," (mutter mutter) "unscrew, and they give one last pull, blood starts pouring. It all ... 's like a fountain. I'm watching myself lying there, and ... white as the sheets they've put me on."

"Is that your dream? Last night's, or do you have it often?"

"Then I'm sinking through the bed, and I'm in the sea, and Dad's with me, and there's all sorts of people ... teeth like sharks, everyone's tearing everyone else's eyes out ... falling all over the place, putting all the eyes in a pot for their tea..." He trailed off.

"Do you talk to them? Say, Stop tearing each other's eyes out?"

"I say, Tear *their* eyes out, them up there, them with their locks and their keys." So I was right. His father was in a nut-house.

I could see the place now, along on the right: huge, red brick, with rows and rows of identical windows, the top ones with bars on. Well, if you were in there you'd want to throw yourself out, wouldn't you? And a tall chimney with smoke coming out. It reminded me of one of those Nazi places, honestly. Did I have to go in there with him? What was I going *for*?

"Look, Vern," I said. "Hang on a minute. What's happening? What d'you want me to do?"

"Needn't come if you don't want."

"I don't know if I want to or not, I just want to know what I'm supposed to be doing there."

We were at the gates, huge wrought-iron things, open, with great brick gateposts.

I stopped. Vern stopped for a second, then he turned and went along the drive. It had tall dark trees on each side, with rhododendron bushes behind, then at the end of the drive some great big steps and a massive oak front door.

I watched Vern getting smaller. I didn't know what to do. If I walked back the way we'd come, there'd be a bus stop, wouldn't there? I could catch a bus back into town.

Some people came walking along, carrying bright flowers and bags of shopping. They looked perfectly ordinary, and they turned in through the gates and went up the drive.

Chicken, are you? I went after them and in through the huge door.

There was a reception desk behind a window, and I said to the girl – she had a sun-dress on, not even a uniform – "That boy - where did he go?"

"Vern?" she said. "Upstairs, first floor – his dad's moved down since he last came."

I set off up the stairs. They know him well, call him Vern. The girl's friendly, I'm allowed in.

On the first floor landing, there was Vern sitting on one of a row of grey school-type chairs. Like that clinic. I sat down too.

"What're you doing here? Can't you find your dad?"

"See Sister. Got to wait." He jerked his head

towards a corridor going off behind us.

"Have to get permission, do you?" Other people were coming upstairs and going straight in through the double doors marked Wards 3 and 4.

"See about 'im coming out."

Footsteps came down the corridor, then a starchy middle-aged Sister woman was standing in front of us.

"Good afternoon, Vernon," she said. "Brought your girlfriend with you today, have you?"

Vern didn't say anything. We'd better not get into any misunderstandings. "I'm just a friend, Sister," I said, using my best middle-class tones. "I was coming this way, so I thought I would accompany Vern. How is his father?"

She turned to me as if Vern wasn't there. "Up and down, you know, up and down. We do have our ups and downs, but we get used to them. The doctor's trying some different medication, and we seem to be doing quite well with it at the moment."

"Is there any chance of him coming out in the near future, do you think?"

"Well, that all depends, doesn't it. It depends on where he's to go. With his history of rent defaulting, there's not much chance of another tenancy, is there? Not in the current climate."

"I'll get somewhere," Vern said. It sounded like a threat.

"Yes, Vernon, we know you will." Yes, little dog, we know you want your bone. "The question is – where, and when? We've offered him a hostel –" she turned to me again, away from the dog – "with a warden in charge, very suitable in his sort of case.

Community care, we're very keen on it. But he's stubborn, very stubborn indeed, Miss Er –"

"Marquis. Sister, I can assure you that Vernon will find a solution in due course. He's a very determined young man." Grandmother Moses, what kind of female am I turning into? I improvised a social worker with the GCSE drama lot: I was good.

"Oh! Er… You've been seeing your social worker regularly, have you, Vernon? Perhaps…" She looked at me again. I'd put her in a total dither. "I'm sorry, they get younger every day, I never know who's a social worker and which is a client."

"As I said, I'm just a friend," I said coolly. "So it will be possible for his father to leave hospital as soon as suitable accommodation is arranged?"

"Of course. His section has been over for some time."

Section? What's she on about? I wasn't going to let her think I didn't know the jargon. "And it's all right to visit him now?"

"Of course, of course. In you go. And if you will, er, let us know the address and the name of a person who would be responsible for his welfare? All right, Vernon? Goodbye, Miss – er – " And she was off back down the corridor. Vern got up. He didn't look at me, he stood looking at the doors.

"Not bad, eh? I can really put it on when I try, can't I?"

Was he waiting for me to come in with him?

"Look, I'll wait out here, if you don't mind. You'll want to have some time on your own with him."

He waited another second, then shrugged his shoulders and went in through the double doors.

Chapter 12

I'm not waiting for Sister Patronise to come back, that's for sure.

I was just about to hop it down the stairs – but my feet turned back. Should I just take a peek through the windows of those double doors – see if I can see him – Vern's dad?

There was no one around so I went up and put my nose practically against the glass. I was expecting to see rows and rows of beds, but it wasn't like that. There were alcoves with armchairs - two men playing draughts at a table – women with handbags, visitors I suppose, sitting with cups of coffee and talking to men. Like a scruffy hotel.

Past all those people I could see the unmistakable giraffe-like back of Vern.

Then a man's face suddenly appeared from nowhere in front of my eyes. I got such a shock I forgot he was behind the glass and thought he was going to shove his face right into mine. His hair came right down over his face but his eyes gleamed through it, and when he saw me he grinned a wide toothy grin, like one of those gibbons Vern was so neurotic about at the zoo.

A burly male nurse in uniform loomed up, "What's this, Tom – scaring the visitors, are we?" and dragged him away. He turned back to stare at me as he was hauled off and he was still grinning.

Quick – away. Down the stairs.

But before the gibbon came, I'd seen Vern's dad.

Just a glance, but that was enough. He wasn't like the gibbon. He was talking to Vern and he looked just like him except his body was bulky, and his face – talk about animated! He looked like he'd take off into outer space with animation. It was bizarre, coming out of that face – an exact older version of deadpan Vern.

He was like a caged animal – gentle, desperate.

My trainers squeaked down the stairs. Mustn't think about Vern, Vern's dad. Got to think about me.

As I got to the bottom of the stairs I said to myself, "Splendid work with Sister Patronise, Miss Marquis. GCSE Drama Grade A, without a doubt. If only your parents'd had the sense to let you to go in for it." I went and said to the girl at reception, "Tell Vern I'll be waiting for him just out there, will you?" and swung my bag casually as I wandered down the drive.

I turned off to the right through the row of trees, and just as I was meandering past the rhododendrons I shouted, "Hell and damnation!" Bit my lip – didn't want them dragging me back in there for a patient. "Why *didn't* they let me take Drama? Why stop me doing the one subject I'm ace at?"

The picture of Vern's dad came back but I shoved it away again. Dad's got a Thing against acting – "Don't put your daughter on the stage Mrs Worthington" – he whines on about eighty-five per cent of actors being unemployed at any one time – "All the travelling – the stress – actors with their massive egos…" You don't get ego-trips in a bank, do you? People who work in insurance never suffer from stress? That's what they want me to be – some crummy clerk with painted fingernails number-crunching on a computer all day.

I flung myself down on the grass in the sunshine and stared up at the blue. Mouthed all the swear words I could think of – and that was quite a lot.

Imagine me up on stage, famous as Meryl Streep, getting my Oscar, saying "Told you so" to old Dinwiddie and Mum and Dad. To Dad more than anyone. He works night and day in the theatre, for the theatre, doesn't he? Then why does he hate it? I've seen him talking to actors in the bar – he's happy enough then – livelier than when he's at home. But Mum goes on about that wretched place as though he was chief jailer at Broadmoor.

Gibbon Man scared me. My heart's still thumping.

I could see a bit of the drive through the rhododendron bushes and the trees. People were still walking up the drive, and one or two were beginning to walk back down it: they must've had enough of visiting for today, like me.

I turned over, got my dreams out of my bag and started flicking through them. Remembered the first thing Vern had said to me, sitting on that bench staring at the Clifton suspension bridge: "Tame. Pathetic" – meaning my dreams.

Tame? Are they? Seem pretty horrific to me. Hunchbacks and sea-horses – being captured by sailors who turned out to be octopuses – Dad with bloody hands, Mum drowning in mud…

Not as violent as his, though. Vern's dreams really are violent: blood draining out of his legs, eyes getting torn out and eaten for tea – that's cannibalism. He's infecting me. That's it: he's infecting me with the bloodiness of his dreams.

I'm scared of him. I'm scared of him, and I'm fond

of him, and I want to be quit of him, and I want to stay with him, and he's totally irrelevant in every way, and I'm madly curious about him. And now there's his dad. Vern's dad's turned from a phantom into a human being. I don't like it.

If I wander off and get a bus back into town, I need never see Vern again. If his dad's insane, Vern's probably fairly insane himself. He'll infect me with his madness like he's infected me with his bloody dreams.

So, I'll go back to Mum and Dad, will I, and be a good little obedient Bean – baked to a turn, just how they like me? Yah.

Through the trees I could see a man pushing a barrow along the drive. He'd got a small garden fork and he started taking out rough bits of grass from the edge of the drive. He moved incredibly slowly, zombie-ish, as if he'd been a patient in there since before the Flood and they'd finally decided to let him out for some fresh air.

Will Vern notice me from the drive when he comes out of the hospital? Do I want him to see me?

I'll leave it to Fate. If he sees me I'll stick with him. If he doesn't then he'll go out of my life for ever. Hey, though! Supposing...

No!

But honestly, if he...

A tiny weeny hint of a plan began to tinkle at the back of my brain like a triangle at the back of an orchestra.

I could see him. He was walking nearly as zombie-like as the man with the barrow. Head down, feet in their ruined trainers slopping along. Typical.

He walked on out of my view.

"Vern! Over here!"

He's gone. So. That's it.

No he hadn't. He was walking back – now he was coming past the bushes at a half-run.

He stopped a little way away from me and fell down on the grass and hid his face in his arms. He wasn't laughing this time, he was crying.

Stymied. What should I do? I can't put my arms round him as if he was a baby – he'd freeze, or throw me off. But I can't just sit here and watch him.

Eventually I edged nearer to him and said, "What happened? Is he miserable? Can't you get him out?"

His shoulders went on shaking.

I said, "It must be awful." He'll turn on me at any minute – tell me I don't understand – it's all my fault. What about my plan? Chuck it away. You can't make a suggestion like that when someone's as upset as this.

He came up on to his elbows and started beating his fists on the grass. "I'll do it I'll do it I'll do it – they can't I won't let them I won't let... 'S hiding he's hiding he's hiding ... only comes out for me... 'S crying, he's crying inside..."

His head went down again and he cried and cried and cried.

I edged a bit nearer still. What to do? What if he goes on like this for ever? Should I go to the hospital and...? And fetch Sister Patronise. No.

He rolled over and his face landed in my lap. His face was on my knees and I could feel the wet of his tears coming through my jeans, first on one knee that didn't have a patch on it, then on the other that did.

I should stroke his head, but how can I do a thing

like that? His shoulder? I stared at his thin purply-grey T-shirt and his shoulder-blades heaving underneath. I took one hand off the grass and put it on a shoulder-blade, and said, "Something'll work out, you'll see." I sounded like a cross between Woody Allen and Mary Poppins. But he didn't jerk away, he didn't move except for shaking.

The shaking got less, then his shoulders were still. He rolled over, away from me, and lay there, face hidden in his arms. My knees were cold where his tears had made my jeans wet.

I said, "Isn't there anywhere he can go? Shouldn't he go into one of those hostels? Wouldn't it be better than being cooped up like an animal in that place?"

He turned over and stared at the sky. His face was streaked: he hadn't washed this morning like I had.

"I mean, it'd be a start, wouldn't it? If he was there, some social worker person would help him to get a flat or a bedsitter or something. There's bedsitters and lodgings and stuff near where I live – the actors who come to the theatre move in and out of them all the time. You have to be in the right place at the right time, you hear there's a place going, then you grab it."

He sat up and took a piece of mud-coloured rag out of his pocket and wiped his face. Spat on it, then wiped it again.

"You going home, then?" His voice was a bit croaky.

"God, I thought you were never going to speak again."

"Are you?"

"Don't know. I can't decide. I want to tell them I'm going to Drama School, but I can't stand the look on

121

their faces, the thought of their whining voices saying it's not a suitable occupation for their darling daughter."

"'S your house like? Mansion? Swimming pool in the garden?"

"You nuts? It's…" Well, with Mum's income as well as Dad's, and stretching things to the limit for the mortgage, I suppose it was a bit of a mansion, from a tramp's viewpoint. "It's detached, newish, got four bedrooms. Well, three and the tiny one we shove visitors in. It's not as big as Cal's. Her dad's in Securities."

"Police?"

"No! Money – stocks and shares – that sort of thing."

"Can I come?"

"What? *What?*"

"Come. 'S it far?"

Uncanny. It was my plan. "Er – no. Hour and a half on the train. You mean, you want to come? And stay? What for? How long?"

"Rest."

Yes, that's it. It must wear you out, living rough. "They'd think it was ever so peculiar. They'd see it as My Great Romance." I grinned to myself. That was what'd taken my fancy when the plan struck me: I could just see them standing there, mouths opening and shutting, looking at me bringing home this strange new boyfriend, knowing that nice people are polite to their daughters' boyfriends when they're thrust in front of their noses but – how can you be polite, darling – or, well, be *anything* – to *this* one? Vern'd make Chris look like the Angel Gabriel.

"Yes, you could," I said. "In fact, I was just thinking, it would be very convenient for me if you came along. If you were there, they'd think…" I couldn't say, You'd give them such a shock that it'd come as small fry when Darling Bina said she wanted a career on the stage. "I think I'd feel happier if you were around. They couldn't be rude to me in front of a stranger."

"What'd you say? 'Bout why I was there?"

That's a thought. "I'll just say 'This is Vern'. I'll be all tight-lipped. Make them beg for information. I'll give it to them – tiny morsel by tiny morsel. First I'll divulge that I went to Bristol – they'll know that already if they're bright enough – then I'll say I went to this Bed and Breakfast – then I looked for a job… All true things, but nothing they really want to know. If they start probing, I'll just glance over at you and they'll think…"

He started to laugh. Hey, I thought, he's only laughed once, hysterically, underneath the cliff. He's never chuckled, or giggled, or even smiled. This laugh now's a bit hysterical, but it's a proper laugh. Then he stopped and said, "Great. Great."

"Look," I said. "One thing they'll think is really weird. People like my parents are always carrying stuff around. Mum's got her handbag – and now she's got her executive briefcase as well, for work. Dad's got his briefcase plus piles of extra papers in brown folders. Going away for a night they need a furniture van. You must have got some stuff. Where is it?"

He put his head down on his knees. That's it, he's realized it's not possible.

He suddenly got up. "Get the bus after me. See you

at the station." And he made off.

I got up and shouted, "What – ? Vern! Wait! What d'you mean?" – and ran hell-for-leather after him.

He stopped and turned round just before the drive. "Station. See you. I'm off, you get next bus." Turned round and off. Loony. He's an absolute utter loony.

I sat down under a rhododendron bush and thought, And so am I, loony. I ought to knock on the door of this hospital and say, Let me in.

Well, so I'm going to meet him at Temple Meads and we're going to set off to the Marquis family abode.

I was terrified out of my wits at the very idea.

I'll ring Cal. Bless her cotton socks for coming back from Spain. That's what I'll do, I'll ring Cal.

I'll say – Cal, I've got sort of attached to this weirdo and he's coming home with me. Nothing in it, just got attached. What? – no, of course I haven't! It's just – I want to go home and tell them to shut up about the exam results and let me do my own thing and leave me alone. Only I'm scared. It may not come out right. This bloke, this weirdo, his father's shut up in a mad-house and I'm scared they'll do that to me. (No, I won't say that. I never told Cal about the clinic.) Can we come to your house first? Your folks know me, I get on all right with them, your mum's a real hoot, I always giggle with your mum, she thinks life's a laugh. Your dad won't be there, will he? No, even if he's there he won't join in, he'll think this is women's business. So – can we come? Then can I ring Mum and Dad from your place – invite them round, maybe? But give us a good meal first, won't you – I haven't had good home-cooking for... for two and a half days. It isn't the cooking, it's knowing the meal's going to be there. I want to come home, Cal, and I don't want to come home, and... You will be there, Cal, won't you, and listen to me?

Looked at my watch: 16.13. No idea what time Vern set off for the bus, but it must be time for the next one by now. What's he going to do between now and meeting me? I'd better set off, or I won't be there at the station and he'll think I'm not coming.

Chapter 13

I didn't take the first bus, or the second. I waited for three buses to go past before I got on to one. I couldn't face sitting at the station waiting for him to turn up: I was damn well going to make him wait for me. If he came at all.

He was there. And he'd washed his face, and changed his T-shirt – this one was sort of greyish-yellow. He was standing beside a time-table, drooping like a question mark. Why was he coming? He'd got some internal engine – it drove him, it had its own reasons, it propelled him and off he went. Did he know the reasons himself? He certainly didn't think I needed explanations. He didn't even look at me as I walked over to him. He was holding a crumpled plastic carrier bag with some fashionable logo on it – presumably he'd got it out of a dustbin. What was inside it? It was quite full.

I went to the ticket office and he followed. I asked for one ticket and paid for it, then I watched him ask for the same and fish down inside his carrier bag and bring out a ten pound note. I wondered how much more he'd got stashed away in there.

It was nearly six o'clock, and we'd got forty minutes to wait. My stomach said it was eating time again, so I told him to buy a couple of pies and some biscuits while I went to phone someone. I realized I hadn't told him anything about Cal except about the villa and Harry. Well, I'd fill in the blanks as we went along. Would he fill in his blanks? Doubt it.

I summoned up Cal as I was dialling. Her hair would have got blonde streaks in it from the sun. She'd've been lying on Spanish beaches with her eyes tight shut knowing that every Spanish boy who passed would fancy her. (No, it'd been raining.) Cool, Cal was. Never let them think she knew they fancied her. Innocent – and so they fancied her all the more. I'd watched it happen at school.

It was Cal that answered the phone. When she heard my voice she gasped, then collapsed into giggles. I could hear her mum in the background – "Cal, who is it? It isn't Robina – it can't be Bina?" I said, "Shut up, Cal – give me your mum, I'll get some sense out of her." So her mum came on, and I said, "Mrs Fry, I'm sorry to bother you, but…" and she said, "Bother? Don't be ridiculous, Robina. What can we do for you?" Amazing – not even, "Where are you?"

I told her I was scared to go home but I thought I ought to, and of course she said, "You'd be best to come here, then, and when you feel like it, we can phone your parents and tell them whatever you want them to know. Robina –" she laughed her little infectious laugh – "you haven't done anything … silly, have you?" I said "What do you mean?" in such shocked tones she believed me straight away.

Now – how was I going to tell them about Vern? I asked to talk to Cal again. She'd stopped giggling and she said, "Tell me all." So I came out with my speech about this weirdo, nothing in it et cetera et cetera, and then the money ran out and I got her to ring me back and I said it all over again (nothing in it…) and she hooted and said, "I'll bet. Thought you hadn't got over

Chris yet!" Hope her mum wasn't listening – no, she would've gone into the kitchen to cook poor Bina a nice meal. Didn't want Mrs Fry knowing about Chris, the way she felt about boyfriends, not if I was bringing Vern along.

It took me about quarter of an hour to sort it all out, and then she asked what train and said she'd get her mum to agree to "take in this 'Vern' or whatever his name is" and meet us at the station.

"You won't tell Mum and Dad, will you? Till I ask you to?"

"Would I?" No, she wouldn't. What's more, nor would Mrs Fry. They should make more of them like that.

Scene: a railway compartment. Dum-a-di-dum, dum-a-di-dum. Pale spiky girl one side of a table, pale pasty boy the other.

Script: she speaks. He doesn't answer. She speaks again. Silence.

She speaks again, chattily this time, about her friend Cal and how nice it'll be to see her again, and she hopes that he'll be polite and help with the washing up.

Silence.

(Nigel, darling – all screen writers seem to be called Nigel – I don't think this comes up to your usual standard of screenplay. One can take mystery a little too far – no?)

I had an idea. I got the exercise book out of my bag and tore the middle two sheets out. I wrote: "These are the questions that really bug me about you. Please will you reply, otherwise I will leave you on the station and tell my friend's mother that you are not coming with

128

me after all. Number One: Are you on the run from the law? Yes/No. Number Two: If I borrow anything from you, will I be receiving stolen property? Number Three: Have you got your own personal cave up there on the cliff? Number Four: What do you think you're going to get out of coming with me?" And slid it across the table.

No reaction.

"Well?" I was just about to offer him my pen when he produced one from his carrier bag: a grotty looking biro with a chewed end. So he could write.

Within three and a half seconds he'd made a couple of marks on the paper and shoved it back.

Number One: a ring round the "no". Number Two: blank. Number Three: ring round the "yes". Number Four: blank.

He grabbed the paper back, scribbled something else and shoved it over to me again.

Number Three: "You'd never find it.".= Number Four: "Learn the lingo." Scrawly writing, quite legible.

"Lingo?"

"Like you at the hospital," he said. "Gets you places. Looks don't count – lingo does."

I thought about it. Yes: when Paul Braithwaite (High School's record-breaking delinquent) makes excuses to Mr Beddowes (deputy head) he's told it's "insubordination". Amanda Farrar (got thrown out of three independent schools, so forced to come to our place) gets Mr Beddowes to simper and smarm to Dinwiddie about her deprived childhood.

I grinned. "Right. We'll do a *Pygmalion* on you and you can go back to the hospital and charm them into letting your dad out."

"Pig what?"

For the rest of the journey I told him the plot of *My Fair Lady*.

My heart was doing its usual bass drum act as we drew in. What if Cal's mum wouldn't have Vern in the house – if Dad went and had that heart attack – if Vern started acting super-weird or stole the family silver...

The familiar platform. A hundred years since I was here. Maybe the man at the ticket barrier'll say, "Hey, love, what have you done to that beautiful hair of yours?"

Cal was standing there, anxiously running her eyes over each of the carriages, looking for me.

I jumped off and ran towards her and ... she backed away. God! I stank!

No – it was just, "Your hair! Bina, you've been and gone and done it!"

I said, "You're brown, you beast!" Then "Here's Vern." He didn't put out a hand but Cal grabbed his free one and said, "Glad to meet you, Vern. Bina's told me all about you." He was all limp, so she sort of frowned at him, decided to ignore him, and put her arm through mine. We started walking off, Cal saying, "Your folks are beside themselves, they can't stop going on about how desperate they are, your mum's sure your dad's going to have a..." I turned round: Vern was following on like a dog.

Mrs Fry was at the barrier. She's got lots of curly brown hair with a little heart-shaped face in the middle, and her smile was so big that it nearly disappeared into the curls at each side. "Robina!" she said, and gave me a big hug.

"Mum!" said Cal. "Her hair!"

"Oh yes – you've done something to it – wasn't it a bit longer? And you must be, er – Vern. Hello, Vern." Cal must have told her there was Nothing In It, I just felt sorry for him, she'd got to be kind and take him in, only for a night. Mrs Fry was kind, she helped at the WRVS.

Vern put his hand out this time. Mrs Fry shook it gingerly and said, "You must be dying for something to eat, both of you. We usually eat at seven, but we waited for you – I've got a casserole in the oven."

Casserole! I'd forgotten casseroles existed.

We got to the Volvo – "Your things? Oh, you've only got a little bag each" – and climbed in. Vern must be thinking he'd really made it. I wanted to dig him in the ribs and tell him that Mrs F was the last of twelve children in her family and her father'd been a maintenance man on the railways. Which was true, though Mr F's father was a Brigadier.

All the instantly recognizable roads, houses, trees. It's like a toy town I've put away in the cupboard because I'm too old for it and here it is, still waiting for me.

"Did you come back from the villa specially for me?"

Cal didn't turn round from the front seat, but Mrs Fry said, "We couldn't go on playing Scrabble in the rain when we knew you'd gone off like that, and your parents sounded so dreadful on the phone. Could we, Cal?" She laughed.

"No, Mum. We couldn't." Odd – she didn't laugh. In fact, she sounded cowed. They hadn't … there wasn't a plot between…?

"It's nice Robina found you, Vern," Mrs F said over her shoulder. "How was it that you met?"

"Sort of – casually." I was a bit breathless, hoped they wouldn't notice. "Beside the SS *Great Britain* – d'you remember me telling you about going there with Mum once, Cal, ages ago, when we lived in Exeter? Vern's father was in the Merchant Navy – he's been everywhere."

"Everywhere?" Cal turned round for the first time and stared at Vern. "Where's everywhere?"

"'Stralia. Japan. South 'Merica."

"Where is he now, then?" Cal despised him. Well, of course. She never met Chris, but she thought he sounded terribly romantic. I hadn't told her he was five foot two – she mightn't have believed he was romantic anyway.

What would Vern say about his dad? Of course: nothing. I chipped in, "I stayed in this elegant Bed and Breakfast place in Bristol and..."

"Bristol? Your mum guessed it was Bristol, she went down the list of codes in the telephone book."

"Did they think of coming to get me? I thought they might get in the car and..."

"No," said Mrs Fry. "We asked them if they were going, and they said it would be pointless to roam all over Bristol, it was such a huge place and... We offered to go ourselves, didn't we, Cal." I could tell by the tone of her voice: Mrs F could see it too. Mum and Dad didn't care.

"Oh!" I suddenly remembered Cal's results. "Congrats on your exams, Cal." She'd opened her mouth: what about *my* results? "Don't say anything – you're not to say a single thing. Forbidden. No-go area."

"OK." She turned back. "In Spain —"

"The villas were half empty," her mum interrupted her. "Really, it's been a terrible season, rain rain rain, you can't help feeling sorry for the trades people, they have to live all winter on what they get from tourists."

There was something funny going on. Cal and her mum were hardly speaking to each other. If there was so much rain, how come Cal was brown? Her mum was brown too. My heart started playing drums again. We were turning the corner into their road. Will Mum and Dad be waiting for me in the hall? What about Cal's dad? Will the Frys lay into me, send Vern off into the night, tell me I need my head examining making friends with *that* sort of boy?

Into the drive, out of the car and into the house. No one in the hall except the grandfather clock I'd seen floating in my dream; no one came out of the sitting room. Thank god, Mr F must be out. There was no one else: Cal's two older brothers worked away – one was something in The City.

Mrs Fry went straight to the kitchen, told us to sit down at the table, opened the oven (split-level cooker, of course) and got out a huge pot. Took the lid off, and it bubbled. I reeled at the smell. Sneaked a look at Vern – he looked smug.

Cal said, "You'll want to wash your hands?" looking at Vern.

"Oh yes," I said quickly. "You go to the downstairs one, Vern – it's just along there on the left. I'll go up to the bathroom."

When I came down there was a slosh-slosh sound coming from the downstairs cloakroom. He must have realized that cleanliness goes along with posh lingo.

When we were all sat down and Mrs F was serving out the stew, I ignored Vern and decided to take the situation into my own hands. DO IT DO IT DO IT – that was what the dream had said.

"I think I know why I flunked my exams," I said between huge mouthfuls. "It's because I was trying to tell myself something, and I wasn't taking any notice. If you know what I mean."

"Yeah – Mum, I told you, didn't I –" Cal suddenly got excited – "it's because Bina's not allowing herself to be what she ought to be! Didn't I, Mum?"

"Cal! What did you say I ought to be?"

"An actress, of course."

"Of course? How long have you thought that?"

"For ever and ever. But you always said 'No one with any sense goes on the stage, you spend most of your time on the dole'."

"That was just parent-speak! I was only saying what Dad says! How can I have said that? It's ridiculous! If you've got to act, you've got to act, there's no *sense* about it, it's a question of something inside you compelling you, not letting you do anything else – the stage is your life, you don't care about pay or conditions or –" I dried up. I'd stopped eating.

"Well," said Mrs Fry. "That's that, then, isn't it," and she laughed. She turned away to get something out of the fridge, which turned out to be a glass bowl full of trifle. Then she said, still with her back turned, "Have you any idea, Robina, why your parents are so against you going on the stage?"

134

I started to eat again and mumbled, "Not the faintest. I know Dad says he knows all about the theatre because he works there, but he doesn't, he doesn't know a thing about actually being out there on the boards – waiting in the dressing rooms for your call – putting on your make-up – rehearsing in a real ensemble where you do workshops and Stanislavsky method and... He only knows about money, Arts Council grants, stuffy councillors going on about 'bums on seats'."

Cal said, "See, Mum! I knew it all along."

I was mad with her. "Then why didn't you say so?"

"'Cos I thought it was a daft idea. There's no money in it, you have to travel around, never settle and have your own home. What about getting married and having children?"

Children! Cal was thinking about having children, when she can act nearly as well as I can! I know I was a brilliant Bottom but you should have seen her Titania. "So I have to fail all my GCSEs so I can find out what you knew all the time?"

"That's right – blame me. Look, Bina, what have you been doing these last few days? Wandering around, sitting in a daze thinking about the Future, picking up ... ideas, making friends..."

Here we go: Please explain Vern. "Just wandering, really. Vern was wandering too, so we sort of got talking. Didn't we, Vern?"

Vern was getting some more stew ladled on to his plate by Mrs F. "Talked about dreams," he said.

"Dreams?" Cal glared at him as though he'd said Pornography.

I said rapidly, "I've been having these dreams. We

135

got on to dreams because Vern's interested in them too. They're psychologically fascinating, aren't they? D'you know you can talk to your dreams – ask them questions?"

Now Cal looked at me. She'd begun to wonder if I was a bit touched too. "Oh, can you? Do they answer you back?"

"Mine don't," I said, airily. "Do yours, Vern?"

He'd gone back to his stew, and silence. Cal pursed her mouth at me. I'd have to find some way of talking to her alone. I couldn't have Cal thinking this creature had anything to do with me – I'd have to explain I was only using him to threaten Mum and Dad with.

There crawled into my mind one nasty little question that I'd been fighting off till now. How am I going to get rid of Vern when he's no more use? The clock chimed in the hall: it must have done it several times but I hadn't heard.

"Now," said Mrs Fry, "trifle, anyone? Don't hurry with your stew, er – Vern. Have some trifle, Bina – I can see the glint in your eyes. Afterwards, shall we have some coffee in the sitting room and talk about when and how we'll get in touch with your parents?"

Chapter 14

"Tell them to bring Bri," I said. "Brian'll say something stupid and we'll all have to laugh." They wouldn't want to bring him – they'd think he should be "protected". Well, I'd refuse to speak to them if he didn't come.

Mrs F thought it should all be intimate. "Are you sure you want us there as well, Robina?"

Hell's teeth, intimacy's the last thing I want. I can see me getting reduced to the old snivelling Darling. Anyway, the bigger the audience the more likely I can be in charge. "Absolutely sure."

"And Vern?"

"Of course."

In the pauses, I tried totting up the words Vern had spoken since we'd arrived. I got as far as nine. At the moment he was sitting in Mr Fry's big armchair with the shelves full of nick-nacks behind him. He was swigging hot chocolate, his tatty carrier bag on one side of him and the tin of biscuits on the other. I stopped being embarrassed about him and thought, You did right, Beano, bringing him. There'll be no tears, no How can you do this to us! not with him here. I exaggerate, of course: they don't go in for tears, they just ignore me.

"Look, Mum," said Cal. "Shouldn't we get it over with? Can't you go round there now?"

"Let me get this absolutely straight, Robina." Her sweet face was crumpled like a screwed-up paper bag. "You want a sort of conference. No one is to interrupt anyone, especially you. If they listen properly and say yes to what you want, you'll come home."

"Remember to tell them about the hair," Cal added. "And the boyfriend."

"He's not my…!"

"OK, OK. But –" (she was just about to say "warn") "tell them about him, anyway."

I said, "Just say he's a friend. All right, Vern?" Vern hadn't even reacted. You could talk about him as if he wasn't there.

At last Mrs Fry went off round the corner to our house. I wished I could be a fly on the wall. No I didn't.

The minute she'd gone Cal grabbed my hand, held it till the front door banged shut, plus another minute to see if her mum would open it again to shout "But what do I say if they ask – ?" Then she took a quick look at Vern and said to me, "You must come and see my photos, Bina. They're upstairs. Make yourself at home, Vern – eat as many biscuits as you like."

As she hauled me up the stairs I braced myself for "What the blazes, Bina? Who is this creep? What in hell's name do you think you're doing?" etc. etc.

But she didn't. She shut the door and said, "Bean, thank God you're here. I thought I'd die. Just die. Sit there. Where's my photos. I had them processed at the one-hour place, cost me a fortune but… He's called Frederico. They're trying to stop me ever seeing him again. But we'll manage something – he's going to write – I've given him your address, Bina – when you get a letter from Spain it'll be to me from him – you will hide them from your parents, won't you? Oh, you can't think how relieved I was when you phoned…"

138

"Cal! You mean it wasn't the rain – you didn't fly back because of me? It was all about you, and… What did you say his name was?"

"Frederico. Look. Here he is."

Out with the photos. "But – he's about thirty-five!"

She snatched it back. "Twenty-seven. Don't be like that, Bean – that's what *they* say – 'He's sure to have a wife and seven kids back in Madrid.'"

My head wanted to burst into tiny pieces on her bedroom floor. I've got to decide what I'm going to say to Mum and Dad – I've got to picture them, feel what they always make me feel like and somehow change it … speak to them like speaking to a dream, make it my dream instead of their dream… And here's Cal spilling this Victorian melodrama all over me, and I'm rivetted. Her parents are OK, yes, but they're strict. Her mum's religious, her dad's religious and tight. Go to discos, but Home by Eleven and No Steady Boys. Mrs F is gentle and sweet and understanding, but…

"D'you remember," Cal said, "when I was new at school when you were too, three years ago, they'd taken me away from St Catherine's and I never told you why. Well, it was this teacher, he fancied me, and they panicked." Cal's the sort that older men go for. Delicate, doll-like. Only she isn't a doll. They realize that eventually. "They think Frederico's like Mr Aldington. Only he isn't. I love him, Bean. I adore him. And he adores me. It's like… Oh hell, it's like all the stupid stories you've ever read. They're true, Bina. It's love. You'll recognize it when it comes to you. Look, that's him on the balcony of the villa. Mum and Dad were on the beach – I told them I was having

139

a siesta."

So much for the rain. Lies. How much of what you get told is lies? I looked at the photo. "He looks like a male model. 'See my Y-fronts'."

"Yes, he could do anything – modelling, acting… He's a courier, with tourists. Of course *they* say he's beneath us."

So what would my "they" say about Vern? Sudden thought: "Where's your dad? Why isn't he here, putting man-proof locks on your doors?"

"Golf club. You know my dad, can't stand rows. Lays down the law, then off to golf and booze."

"And your mum?"

"She's under his thumb. God, she's feeble. She's trying to win me back now, being nice to you and what's-his-name."

I felt cheated. I'd really liked Mrs F. "Cal, you're not pregnant or anything, are you?"

"Course not!"

And sex? I'd never asked her before. I'd thought she was like me, wanting but scared. Anyway, she was above all the lads in our year – she liked stringing them along but she couldn't have fallen for any of them. I knew she fancied Mr Malone, but we all fancy Mr Malone. This Spaniard – twenty-seven years old… "I bet you didn't sit on the sofa with him, holding hands."

"I'm sixteen and a half, Bean." She said it quietly. "And I've always been mature for my age."

I could hear Frederico saying it. Or someone before that? "Was he the first, Cal?" I realized as soon as I said it that I didn't want to hear the reply.

Maybe she didn't hear me. She was gazing at his

photo, and she said, "He's so gentle. He takes care of me, he takes care of everything."

I didn't want to hear any more. "Cal," I said.

"Right," she said. "Tell me I'm a bad girl. Tell me it's not the real thing. But can I come round and use your phone sometimes when your folks are out? I'll pay, honestly – but if they find out —"

"Cal!"

"What?"

"Have I listened to you? Just now – have I listened?"

"I suppose so. Why?"

"Now you've got to listen to me. I can't think about Frederico. I've got to think about me."

"Course you have. But will you give me his letters?"

"Course I will – what d'you think I'd do with them, flush them down the loo?"

"And let me use the phone?"

"Yes yes – *listen* to me, Cal! I need to practise. They'll be here in a minute and I've got to work things out. Will you do it with me? You be them, and I'll be me?"

She heard me at last. We'd done this lots of times, role play, in Soc. Ed. classes and out of them. "OK – sorry. And – sorry and all that about your exams. You should have said. I thought you were all right. Why didn't you tell me? What did you write on all your papers?"

"I haven't a clue – I was freaking out at the time. Brilliant actress – I can totally freak out and not even my best friend knows. Let's get on with it. How long d'you reckon we've got while your mum's round there?"

We gave ourselves ten minutes. I said my say: "It's not that I'm angry with you, or that you've done anything wrong. I just needed to get in touch with my feelings." ("Great, great," said Cal. "That's just the sort of thing your mum says.") "And my feelings are telling me that we've all been wrong about what I want to do. I want to go to Drama School and be an actress." She made me repeat it five times. Oh, it sounded good.

"Say it again with a smile in your voice," ordered Cal.

No problem. "I want to go to Drama School and be an actress."

Still no sound from the front door. "Let's go down," I said.

"What the hell will Vern be doing?"

"Eating his way through our kitchen cupboards, probably. Honestly, Bina, what on earth did you pick *him* up for? Couldn't you have landed someone a bit more..."

"I told you, Cal – he just tagged along, and I thought he'd be good ammunition against Mum and Dad."

"But what do you see in him? And what do his parents think – him going off to a distant town with a stranger like you?"

"I don't know much about him. You don't ask Vern things like that. He's a one-off." I'm not going to go into the dream thing with Cal, or say anything about Vern's dad. If she says anyone's a head case, she means avoid them like the Bubonic Plague. *He was like a caged animal – gentle, desperate...* Vern's dad's face hovered in my head like a dream.

"For all I know he'll have disappeared already," I said as we went downstairs. But he was sitting where we'd left him beside an empty biscuit tin.

"Hello," Cal said to him sweetly. "What would you like now? Cereal? Toast? Fruit? Just say the word. We've even got one of Mum's home-baked Christmas puddings left over from last year —"

"Shut up, Cal." I was pacing up and down. (So people actually do pace up and down when they're nervous.)

Cal sat down opposite Vern. "And you live in Bristol, do you?"

Grunt.

"Which part? I believe Clifton's very attractive."

I said, "We met near the suspension bridge."

"Oh, that was where the first magic encounter took place, was it? How did it happen? Your eyes just met, across a crowded river?" She wasn't going to get anywhere. "And your parents? Have they met Bina?"

"Cal, can I have a drink, please? I'm parched."

She put out her tongue at me and went to the kitchen.

I glared down at Vern from above. "Be civil, can't you? You can't just sit there and munch their biscuits without a single bloody word! Help me out, for God's sake!"

Then I heard voices from outside the front door, and the key in the lock. Here they were.

Chapter 15

Mrs F was saying, "And of course she's very tired, so…"

I should go out into the hall. I went and stood in the sitting room doorway, but I couldn't get any further – my legs wouldn't move.

Brian came in first. He looked embarrassed, thinking, why do I have to be in on these crises? I suddenly wondered, why did they send him on that Adventuring course? He's no good at sport. Maybe to improve his image.

Good old Bri, he just looked at me and my hair and said, "It's a porcupine!"

"It's not a porcupine, it's a hedgehog."

"Hedgehogs get fleas."

"My hedgehogs don't."

By that time Dad and Mum were standing in a line with Bri along the hall. I'd forgotten what a thin face Dad had got – how old he was. He's quite good-looking in a film-starry way – I'd always thought of him as young. But now the first thing I saw were the lines on his face standing out like the lines on a charcoal drawing. Mum's the opposite – smooth. Her clothes were smooth, her make-up was smooth, she looked like a picture out of a magazine for mature women. They both looked ghastly white and tense. I'd be sorry for them if I wasn't so scared.

"I'll put the kettle on," said Mrs Fry. She bumped into Cal coming out of the kitchen and they started arguing over who should make the tea.

I said, "Hello, Mum – Dad. What d'you think, then? Hedgehog or porcupine?"

Dad said, "Robina, what the hell…?" and Mum said, "Darling, we've missed you so."

I fled back to the sitting room before they could try and kiss me. They followed. "Darling, Mrs Fry tells us you've brought someone with… Oh."

"Oh," said Dad like an echo.

"This is Vern. Vern – my brother Brian, my mum, my dad."

Vern stood up. Yes, he stood up. He didn't exactly offer his hand, but when each of them put out theirs he allowed his to be taken and dangled slightly. "'Llo," he said. We all sat down.

Dad looked as if he was dying for a cigarette: he gave up smoking two years ago when his secretary-before-last got lung cancer. Mum began to look more at ease. She's used to louts, thugs, layabouts – it's her job: she cuts off the bits that Society doesn't like and paints over the scars. Respect Them As Human Beings is her motto. "Thanks for, er, helping Robina out, Vern." I wasn't frightened any more. I wanted to lash out at them: Vern didn't help me, I don't need anyone to help me – he took me to this boat alone at night and we… He's a thief, a criminal, he nicked my bag and I had to sift through every shit-bin in Bristol till I found my dreams and found out what I ought to've known all along if you hadn't…

But I bit it back. Play your part, Bean.

"I'm sorry I've worried you," I said. "I'm sorry about my results. But I… I'm sure – the exams were telling me something. I've had time to think while I've been away."

"So have we, Robina – so have we!" Dad was white – he couldn't contain himself. "You may think we've been putting pressure on you, but —"

"David —"

"Let me say it, Julia. Strange as it may seem, we've lived rather longer than you, we do know what's —"

I put my fingers in my ears. My speech – I had to make my speech. "I'm not blaming you – you haven't done anything wrong. It's just that I needed to get in touch with my feelings." It's funny talking with your fingers in your ears – you can hear it louder than everyone else can. "I know now that we've all been wrong about what I want to do with my —"

Dad marched over, pulled my hands out of my ears and forced them down to my sides. His hands felt sharp and hard, but he was trembling. Should I give him a knee where it hurt? My god, though – this'd be a pretty good scene. It's as if we're rehearsing it: what's my next line? "Robina," he shouted, "we can't possibly discuss anything at all if you persist in —"

Mrs F came in with the tea. Cal followed her and sat on the floor. Dad flushed and let go of me and went to sit down again.

"I'm going to put sugar in everyone's," announced Mrs Fry with a little nervous laugh. "We all need it."

"David, please don't lose your temper," Mum said. She sounded amazingly calm, almost cold. "We've got to explain." This was the middle of an argument they'd begun at home.

"I think it's Robina who's got to explain," said Dad. His voice was as thin as his face, like he was being stretched.

"She was trying to," said Mum. "We must let her –"

It burst from him then, the thing he really cared about. "What about your *exams*, Robina?"

"David, they don't matt —"

I broke in. "Let me say, Mum. I don't know what happened in the exams. I freaked out. It was —"

"'Freaked out'? What in hell's name is that supposed…?"

"David!" She was treating him like a little boy.

"You've put us through all this… Oh, thanks." Cal gave him his cup of tea, and it broke his thread.

Then Mrs F gave a cup of tea to Vern, and somehow we all turned and looked at him. He was the audience and we'd forgotten he was there. We ought to behave nicely.

"All right, Robina. Say your say." Dad looked down at his tea.

I said it. The whole of it, right down to "Go on the stage and be an actress." Cal looked at me and grinned.

When I'd finished, I didn't look at Mum and Dad, I just stared at the carpet. But Bri said, straight off, "Jumping Bean does it again."

"Bri! Again?"

He came over all confused and said, "You're always doing it. Showing off, hitting the headlines."

Dad had turned away, and Mum and Mrs Fry were looking at each other like conspirators.

"I never knew you were jealous, Bri!"

"I'm not jealous. I'm going to be a racing driver, I don't care what anyone says. I'm just fed up of everyone saying 'Oh you're *Robina's* brother.'"

"Well, Brian," said Dad, "we're not discussing your problems, are we? We're discussing Robina's."

I saw Mum catch Mrs F's eye, and Mrs F said,

147

"Brian, I still haven't washed the dishes. Could you come and help me?"

Bri looked puzzled, but it seemed like a summons. Off they went. Cal got up and said, "Should I…?" but I grabbed her, "No. You stay."

Dad was looking at the fireplace. Mum was looking at Vern. Vern wasn't looking at anything.

Mum said, "We've got to tell her, David."

Dad got up. "If you must, Julia. But the principle remains the same." He started towards the door.

"You're not going, David!"

"Yes, I am. You can come home when you've finished."

"David, sit down. This is as much to do with you as it is to do with me. David – you are not going!"

"Yes, I am." He was at the door. I thought he was going to say, I'm not saying anything more in front of *him*, but no, he seemed to have forgotten all about Vern.

"You're not going home now, any more than you're going to have a heart attack, or lung cancer, or any other fatal illness."

They'd forgotten all about me, too. I stood up and yelled at her, "This is all to do with *you*! You're having some row between yourselves and it's nothing to do with me and you never want to listen to me and —"

"It is!" Mum shouted. She'd stood up too, still holding her cup of tea. "It *is* to do with you, Bina! It's more to do with you than anyone else in the world!"

"It's history, Julia," Dad said very quietly. "It's none of her business."

"It is her business, David."

"I know! I know what it is," I screamed at them. "It's always been that – I've known it all my life – you've never forgiven me for being a girl – that's why you love Bri and you don't love me – you wanted a boy – you always wanted a boy and all you got was a girl – all you got was me!"

In the silence, I saw that Mum's cup was on a tilt and her tea was slop-slop-slopping into the saucer. I looked at her face, and at Dad's. I was excited, thrilled. I've come out with it, I've made the real accusation at last!

But they weren't shocked. I could see it. They were simply surprised. Their faces were a complete blank. Dad's forehead was crinkling into a frown. He came back from the doorway and sat down. Mum stared at him – then she stared at me.

"What?"

"I mean – *Robina!*" I said. They'd got me worried. "It's obvious! Why call me a name like that if you hadn't wanted to call me Robin really? I mean!"

They sat down again. "Oh," said Mum, "my tea. It's spilt." She put down her cup and took a tissue out of her trendy cardigan and started dabbing at her skirt. "Bina, you've got it wrong. I'll explain to her, David." She put the tissue between the saucer and the cup.

There was a noise in the doorway and we all looked up. We hadn't heard the front door opening and Cal's father coming in.

It was a dream I had – *We were wallpapering a wall, Dad and Mum and Bri and me. No – they were wallpapering, and I was the wall —they were papering over me. I was panicking – I'll get stuck between the paper and the wall – I'll disappear! But*

*I glanced behind me and saw – nothing. Where the
wall should be was a space, a mist, a foggy drop into
infinity… And Mr Fry was floating out there in the
mistiness, and he was busy wallpapering too but he'd
got the paper in a mess – he'd put the paste on it and
picked it up paste side nearest and it was sticking to
him. He pushed it away but the more he pushed the
more it stuck to him. The dream flashed across my
mind in bright colour.* Had I dreamt up Mr Fry lolling
there in the rectangle of the doorway? He filled it:
huge, almost squared off at the edges.

He was trying to focus on Vern. "And who may you
be?" Unsteadily.

*The wallpaper was purple and yellow and green
stripes…* But the dream had vanished. I looked at
Mum: what in hell's name could she say next?

She went on speaking as if Mr Fry wasn't there.
"No, you've got it wrong, darling," she said – talking
to me, but every so often glancing across at Dad. "We
love you, we love having a girl. We called you Robina
after a friend of the family because she died when you
were on the way. But – Daddy was an actor in those
days, you see – I was in costumes, we met on *An
Inspector Calls* – and he didn't earn very much, well,
almost nothing in fact, and you were, er, a bit of a
surprise. Actually we weren't married at the time, so
we had to get married straight away and find some
money to buy a house and so on, and Daddy had to
give up acting and find a real job, one that brought in
a regular income. So he knows – we know – we
thought we knew, though of course we may be wrong
– that you shouldn't make the same mistake as he did,
going into acting."

Dad was looking away from her now. I was as sure as anything I've ever been sure about in my whole life that he wished he was still an actor.

"I'm sorry, David. It really needed to be said. Does that make things a little clearer, darling?"

Mr Fry made his way across the room, staring at Vern and swaying. "Who's this creature? Girl's pregnant by him, is she? No self-respect, 's what's wrong with girls these days. Mind you – this creature 's not capable, if you want my frank opinion. This…. madam of ours – 's got herself a greasy Spaniard. God, they're all at it. Not like the days when we were young," addressing Mum and Dad. "What I want to know is, why can't they carry on decently, like we used to do?"

Chapter 16

Chaos. Mrs F burst into tears. "Gordon, how *could* you?" Cal came over to me and said, "Don't they make you sick, parents." Brian bumped into me going across to Vern and – honestly, I could have hugged him – asked him if he knew anything about motor-racing. Mum was saying something to Dad about going home, and he said, "With Robina, or without Robina? And what about *him*?" Mr F lurched into an armchair and shut his eyes.

I was floating above it thinking, Well, *that's* all it was. Mega-scandal – they had to get married on my account. Only ... maybe I ruined their lives and they blame me for it. But I don't feel blamed, I just feel out of it. They've been so busy inventing this non-marriage that they've had no time to notice I really exist. Well, they know I exist now.

Mum took control. "Bina, I think it would help if you came home. Vern – is that short for Vernon? – you're Bina's guest, so you'll be welcome to stay at our house for a night or so..."

"But – " Dad broke in – "as I expect you realize, we can't offer hospitality beyond a limited period."

"Dad!" He was so mealy-mouthed, I couldn't stand it.

"No, he's right, Bina," said Mum. "We've got a lot of talking to do. We need to be on our own, as a family."

Family? What d'you think I needed to escape from? But I can't get out of it, not if I'm going to get what I want. "Is that all right, Vern?" He seemed so far away, such a different animal from these parents of mine, I hardly knew how to talk to him.

"Yeah," he said. "Thanks."

"And you do agree that…" Dad began.

But I stopped him. "Let's go home. I'm clapped out. What's the time?"

It was nearly midnight. Cal clung to me as we left, as if I was her lifeline, but I felt a bit cold towards her. It'd take a while before I sorted out how much I trusted her – where I stood with her. Mrs Fry gave me a weepy hug and said she hoped something would work out for me, she was sure I was full of talent, but… I think she'd known Mum and Dad's secret all along. Maybe Mum confided in her about that, and she confided in Mum about Cal's boyfriends. Was that why Mum was disapproving about Cal? Yes, that figured.

I felt a bit light-headed. How much else was going on that I didn't know about? That's the trouble with finding out the truth at last – you wonder how many more lies there are to come. Maybe Dad's been having affairs with actresses – maybe *Mum's* been having affairs … all those evening classes… I'm not going to think about it. I don't care about them. From now on it's Me for Me. Baked Bean Incorporated, Limited Company.

The sky was clear and there were stars dotted all over it. Mum and Dad walked in front, Brian trotted beside Vern chatting about Nigel Mansell and Alain Prost. I wandered behind thinking how little I knew about stars. I could only identify the Great Bear and Orion – I couldn't even remember which bit of the Great Bear pointed to the North Star. When I'm an actress I'll come out on to the terrace after the show and stand and gaze at the stars and work out which of them I'll still be able to see when I tour America – Australia – take Shakespeare to the Far East. I'll travel like Vern's dad travelled, only with the Royal Shakespeare Company instead of in a however-many-1000-tonne oil tanker.

Has Vern got any pyjamas in his carrier bag? Does he know how to clean the bath after using it? Has he got nits – will we all catch them?

When we got home Mum said, "Well, darling, you'd better go upstairs and show Vern the spare room. There are clean sheets and a duvet in the airing cupboard. Then we'd better get some sleep, all of us. Though I could do with a sherry, David, if you could rustle one up."

I went upstairs and Vern followed. "In there," I said to him, pointing to the spare room. He was more like a giraffe than ever in our perfectly-decorated house – he'd wandered in from the Safari Park and needed showing his way back.

Then I went to the bathroom to fetch the duvet and stuff. The spare room used to seem tiny. Now I remembered the cabin cruiser and this room was enormous.

I should have found a fitted sheet, but this one was the old-fashioned kind that you have to tuck in. I unfolded the sheet and threw one side of it over to Vern. "Pull that bit up to the bed-head and that other bit down to the bottom. Then tuck it in. No, like this: hold this bit here *up*, then tuck this piece under the mattress, so – "

I was tired and confused – I couldn't have expected

154

him to know how to do it properly. Though… "Didn't they teach you to make beds in one of your Home places?"

"Girls did. They tried boys but we all scarpered."

"Oh, tuck it in any old way. You're the one that's sleeping on it. Now the duvet."

I never could put duvets in their covers – it ends up with everything in a twist. "You hold the cover, there at its corners. Now – I put the duvet in here…"

He started to laugh.

"Stop it. Concentrate."

"Wrap me in the cover thing," he said, "an' leave the feath'ry thing on top."

"Hey, that's not a bad idea." And I started to giggle as well. It was like on the hillside, dream time. I collapsed on to the bed and we finished up lying there rolling around laughing our socks off. I had to get up and close the door in case they heard us downstairs – you could be sure they were straining their ears for clues to what was going on.

"What d'you think, then?" I asked when I'd calmed down. "Have I got beastly repressive parents, or are they trying to do their best for their darling daughter?"

"Bloody rich," he said.

"What difference does money make? It's whether they love me or not."

"Makes a difference. I can't get my dad out of that place."

"Yes. Well. D'you reckon they'll let me do it?"

"Course they will. Got to follow the dream."

"But I didn't dream about being an actress!" Or had I? Had he read things into my dreams that I hadn't seen?

"You know. Dreams tell you. Dreams told you."

"They didn't. I told me."

"So. Dreams is you."

It was easy for him. He was disconnected. I wasn't. I was connected to … all this: how to tuck a sheet in neatly, how to pass exams, how to be polite, fit in, not rock the boat. Dreams don't fit in. Dreams rock the boat – can rock it right over, drown you.

"I just wish she'd stop calling me Darling." I sat up. "Vern – who told you about dreams? Your dad?"

"We always dream."

That's why your dad's where he is, I thought. "You've got to be able to tell the difference, though. See where dreams end, real things begin."

"'S what they all say."

"But it's true! Or you live in fairytales! Fantasy! Your feet've left the ground!"

"Them." He jerked his head towards the door. "Them's feet're on the ground. Look at 'em."

"But… Vern, your dad's living in fairytales."

"So?"

So… I went off on a different thought. "It's odd."

"'S odd?"

"Your accent. I've suddenly noticed. You don't talk like a butter commercial. Where did you grow up?"

"'Verywhere. North, mostly. Hull."

We were sitting on the bed with the rumpled duvet in between us, relaxed. "Where did your mother go when she went off – d'you know?"

"Just went. Don't remember."

"How old were you?"

"Sort of … four."

"And it's been just your dad and you? What happened to you when he was at sea?"

"Had an auntie."

"Nice?"

He shrugged. "In the way, I was. Then Dad… Few years back. Got kicked out."

"Of the Merchant Navy?"

"Mm."

"What for?"

Nothing. I didn't look at him. It was too much to expect – I'd gone too far. Then – "'Ggs."

"What?"

"Drugs, 're you deaf? Out on your ear. 'S like that."

Drugs – dreams. "And he couldn't get any kind of job after that?"

"We was together, wasn't we? No harm to nobody. They won't leave a body alone."

"Did you go to school?"

"Whass school for? Got a shelf of books – *No Picnic on Mount Kenya* – ace book that, read it? – *Worst Journey in the World, White Nile. Charles Thingy an' Galapogos Islands* – 's where my dad read about turtles, always had a thing about turtles. Taught me sums, navigation, stars, everythink. School's for stay-at-homes."

I saw Vern's dad's face again, and floated off to where he'd been … seeing to the turbines, the throb of the engine thundering in your ears – watching clouds and star patterns for storms and calm and direction – going on shore leave – bazaars and prostitutes in Shanghai – oil terminals in the sun-dazed Gulf – gabble of men with muscles like ropes unloading mystery cargoes in Rio…

"'Full fathom five thy father lies'," I said.

"What?"

"Shakespeare. *Tempest*. Only he didn't."

"Didn't what?"

"Lie under the sea – his father. He was magicked into drowning, and magicked into seeing his son again. Or he was dreamed into it… 'Such stuff as dreams are made on…'"

"Actress," he said, and stuck his tongue out at me.

"So? That's what I am. Will you come and see me? Seriously? When I'm Cleopatra?"

"Dunno."

No. You don't know where you'll be, or how you'll be, do you? Do I know where I'll be? "I'm going to make it. I'm going to the college and I'll sit some of those bloody exams again, and I'll get there. I'll go to RADA."

"'Ll they chuck you out?"

"What – from home? No. Spoil their image. Have to explain to everyone why I'd left, have to pay for me in some crummy flat. I think they sort of care. Only they've got no time."

"Dad's got time."

"Yes." I felt a great big sigh coming all over me. Almost envy. Then I was afraid for him, more afraid for him than for me. I sort of wished he'd stay, and sort of wished he'd go away. "We'd better go downstairs or they'll think we're having it off up here."

"Having what off?"

He's a child. Cunning like a sneak thief, innocent like a baby. "Nothing. It's half-past midnight. They're waiting to settle us down like good little kiddies. Come on."

Chapter 17

I woke up gently. Did a sound of some kind wake me?
I lay there and listened... Nothing.

I dreamed... I was still half inside the dream. I
dreamt...

At last. I was on the stage. No – not on the stage. In
front of the stage. Not acting. Directing.

*The stage was vast: it was all around me, yet I was
standing in front of it. This theatre had no roof, it was
open to the sky, and the sky was a blanket of stars. I
was standing with my arms held high, and my arms
were long and wide and billowy, like a wizard's, full
of power. I wasn't saying anything, I was bringing the
play into being by the power of my thoughts. Behind
me sat the audience, but they were tiny, and they were
all shaped liked cubes. They were still recognizable as
people.... There was Mr Fry (a big fat cube) and there
was Brian – he was a cube with coloured wavy edges.
But the rows of cubes were miniscule compared with
the stage, which was as big as the universe. There was
nothing, No one on the stage. It was an endless
emptiness.*

*But now there was someone... A girl, or a boy,
coming towards me, carrying something – something
wrapped in a cloth that trailed along the ground as
they approached. I was waving my billowy arms
slowly and hypnotically, and the figure and its burden
were coming towards me in rhythm with the waving of
my arms. Nearer and nearer it came – nearer and
nearer – and I saw that the boy, or girl, was carrying*

an old man. He was as old as if he'd been in the grave for a hundred years, and it wasn't a cloth that was trailing along the ground, it was his beard. His beard was so long that it swept the dusty stage as they came.

I still couldn't see who they were, or whether it was a boy or a girl carrying the old man, but they walked on and on, closer and closer – now they were off the edge of the stage, and floating – and I knew that in a few minutes they would come right up to me – in a moment – in a second...

They'd walked right over me, or past me, or through me as though I was a cloud.

And I was singing in a clear high angelic voice as the old man and his bearer passed beyond me into the starry night.

I lay and gently emerged from the dream. I was splayed out under the duvet – my own familiar duvet, after all that strangeness. I'd had a shower last night and my skin felt silky clean. It was light outside, and quiet: just the hum of an occasional lorry or car from distant roads, and some birds twittering in the trees in the garden.

Well, here's home. I can't remember ever listening to it like this, when it's early morning. I listened to it in the evenings when I went to bed early to be alone. Then you can hear every murmur and creak and raised voice; I even heard Bri tearing out pictures from his motor-racing magazines to stick up on his walls. Will he make it – floppy, unsporty Bri – will he make it as a racing driver? Not a chance. Are they saying that about me: "D'you think Bina'll make it on the stage? Not a chance."

I will. I'll show 'em.

I pulled my knees up and thought about today. I don't want any heavy talking, not till Vern has gone. What'll we do? I could show Vern the town. No – it's Sunday, everything'll be shut. Mum'll try and organize us – though even she couldn't organize a slithery amoeba like Vern. Dad'll bury himself in the Sunday paper. Or maybe they'll spend the day ensconced in their private row.

How about a walk beside the river? Vern'll tell me the names of all the birds and plants. We might find some water rats, or voles, things you never see, you only read about them in *The Wind In The Willows*. Mum used to read that book to Bri night after night till she noticed he always fell asleep in the first sentence.

Time? 6.37. A bit later than we left the boat yesterday. I'll write down my dream.

My barrel-bag was beside the bed, not yet unpacked. My room was just as I'd left it, even to the Agatha Christies and piles of cards on the floor. I got out my exercise book and my pen.

There was something sweet and calm about my dream. I wrote it slowly, savouring it. *Beyond me into the starry night*.

I needed to go to the loo. See if I could get over the landing without creaking the floorboards – I needn't use the flush. No one else'll be awake yet.

I tiptoed to the door and opened it quietly. I went half way across the landing – then stopped.

The spare room door was open. Vern's door.

I tiptoed over to it. He must have left it open 'cos he doesn't like enclosed spaces. (The boat? Backs of cars?) What will he look like asleep? Like a lamb asleep in a field. I put my head round the door.

161

He wasn't there. The duvet was folded on the bed with the cover on top, the pillow beside it. Even the bottom sheet was taken off and folded and put on top of the pillow.

Neat. (Don't leave tracks.)

No plastic carrier bag either. I didn't need to look in the bathroom or downstairs. He'd gone.

March over to the bed – flaming – mad mad mad! He's done it again! Foiled me – fooled me! He's gone for good! Where the hell's he gone to?

Do I care? Of course I bloody care! Not romance or anything crappy like that … just – he was Something, not Nothing! I snatched up the duvet and clutched it. Come back, you loon! Tell me where my dreams are taking me – the next step, and the next, and the next…

There was a crumpling sound from where I was clutching the duvet – a sound like paper. I put the duvet back on the bed, and picked off the cover.

It was a small piece of paper – a hand-out, the sort of thing you get shoved under windscreen wipers in multi-storey car-parks. It was advertising a Sekond Hand KarMart in Montpelier, Bristol, on Saturday 15th August. That was last Saturday, a week ago yesterday.

I could see through the print that there was hand-writing on the back. I turned it over. I didn't recognize the writing – then I did – it was like Vern's scribbled answers to my questions on the train.

I tiptoed back to my bedroom, got into bed and sat up with the piece of paper in my hand and the duvet over my knees, reading.

The writing was scruffy, spidery, with odd letters crossed out. *Monday*. Monday? That must be last

Monday. *Dreemed. Good sweet dreem. Hot. Dads there. House. White, balkny with creepers. Dads sitting. Wine. Smells. Lizerds. Can here gittar, woman dansing – turn and see her along balkny, frilly dress, Spanish. Were eating figs and things off trees. Hill up the back. More houses. Im giving Dad wine. He's smiling.*

I put the piece of paper down on my knee because my hand was shaking. Closed my eyes – pictured the photo of Cal's Frederico on the balcony of their villa.

White, with creepers. Glass of wine in his hand.

Cal had taken the photo from too far away: I wanted to see her Man of Passion in close-up, and all I saw was a tiny figure on a slightly less tiny balcony in the middle of the picture, plus lots of white villa wall, and another house nearby (Mrs Fry complains there's no peace and quiet, they build these villas far too close together) and a slice of rocky hillside in between. And it looked gorgeously, fantastically hot. You bet there'd be lizards (sorry, Vern – lizerds) sunning themselves along that balcony.

I'd forgotten that I needed to go to the loo. I crept to the bathroom and came back. Read it again. "Im giving Dad wine. He's smiling." Vern'd dreamt it six nights ago. Cal, the villa, didn't exist for him then. Cal had only shown me the photos last night, not him, so he couldn't have made it up.

It was eerie.

There was a creak on the landing and a knock on my door. I stuffed the piece of paper down into my bag. "What?"

The door opened and Mum's head came round. "I heard you, darling. Can I come in?" What was on her face? Relief. She thought Vern was in here with me.

"May I?" She sat down on the bed. Not too close. Sort of – shy. "The spare bedroom door seems to be open. I wondered … maybe he likes to sleep with the door open."

"He's gone."

"What?"

"You can look downstairs if you like, but he's gone." She got up. "I'll see." I heard her go across the landing and check the spare room, then go down and into all the downstairs rooms.

Back upstairs. "You're right, darling. Where d'you think he can have gone to?"

"Just gone. He's like that. Mum – please don't call me darling."

"Just – gone? What… Darling? I'm sorry, Bina, does it irritate you?"

"Yes."

"Did you, um, care about him?"

"No. Not like you think. We just sort of picked each other up. Lost souls. I don't suppose I'll see him again."

"I didn't think you had much in common… What, never? Won't you write to him?"

"Don't know where he lives."

"Dar — Bina! You brought him home!"

"Didn't bring him. He came."

She laughed – confused laughing. "Don't tell Daddy, that's all."

"Why not? Why not tell Dad all the nasty stupid crazy things?"

She flushed, really hard, and stared at my barrel-bag on the floor. "Don't talk to me like that, Robina.

It's rude."

"Well, don't call him 'Daddy', not to me. Next May I'm going to be seventeen."

"I know," she said and breathed more ordinarily. "I said to … your father as we were going to bed, we'll have to work this out as between adults."

"I mean it, Mum. About going on the stage."

"I know you do. I've always suspected it. But it's a dreadful life."

"Dad doesn't think so." I wished I hadn't said that: I wanted to keep their row away from me.

"Yes. Well, I had to drag him into the real world, the world of mortgages and telephone bills and mountaineering gear for Brian that cost seventy pounds and was only used for three days. That's how life is."

No, it isn't – needn't be. "I don't think acting's dreadful, I think it's wonderful. And if it's hard, I won't care."

"I saw it, Bina, when I was in costumes. That's why I never went back, that's why I went into Adult Ed. You may not care about the hardships now, but you will in a few years' time when all your friends have got good jobs and —"

"Or they're standing in the dole queue and I'm no richer than they are but at any rate I've got something important in my life."

"Well. We'll see."

That's it. That means I can do it. "I'm sorry, Mum." I did feel sort of sorry, really. "I mean – going off and all that."

"That's all right. I – I knew something had to go, some time." She was talking about her and Dad.

Maybe there *is* more. But it isn't my business. She sniffed and swallowed and said, "We'll manage, don't you worry."

"I'll go to college and get what I need for Drama School. I won't crack up if I'm working for that. Maybe I'll be at Stratford one day."

"Fulfil your wildest dreams."

Dreams. "Mum – don't tell anyone about Vern. It's not anything. Tell Dad it was a freak thing. Forget it."

She got up. "We'll forget the whole thing. We'll go to school at the beginning of term and explain that they did their best but you were going through a bad time and now you're going to the college. So Thank you and Good-bye, as they say."

That's right, Mum – sort me out, just like your delinquents. But I'm not hating her for it. I feel a bit smug. Just get yourself and Dad sorted out. Dad'll never get back on the stage, that's for sure. Maybe me getting famous'll be some compensation. Oh god, no, that'd mean I can't end up as a happy extra on a film set.

We heard noises of Bri on the landing, and Mum said he was missing his friends who were all still Adventuring so they'd agreed last night he could go out on his bike with some Coke and some sandwiches and he needn't be home till late. She said he'd turned out quite good at canoeing and rock-climbing, even though he was useless at football, so maybe there was hope for him after all, and maybe the seventy-pound equipment'd get proper use.

She went off to put on some coffee and toast and do some baking in the kitchen, and I ate toast and honey in front of an ancient film on the telly.

Dad came down in his dressing gown after an hour or more. He got a bowl of cereal from the kitchen and came into the sitting room looking embarrassed. How ridiculous: this man and I have to justify ourselves to each other when (apart from making each other ravingly angry half the time) we're complete and utter strangers. Except (I can hear Mum saying it) we're more alike than either of us dares admit.

"Er – you're set on it, then, are you, Robina?"

"I don't want to talk about it, Dad. Yes, I'm totally set on it."

He turned and went straight out and upstairs to eat his cereal in bed. Defeat. Or: That'll be one actor in the family, at any rate, so – victory?

I went back to Richard Todd as Robin Hood.

About twelve-ish, after she'd been to church to please her mum, Cal phoned. She practically fell on the floor when she heard that Vern had gone. We agreed she should come round in the evening to watch a video (though I knew it was really so she could talk about Casanova Frederico). Her dad'd got a terrible hangover, she said. He was roaring round the house accusing her of giving Frederico one of the keys to the villa because there should have been four of them, one for each and one spare, and she should have put hers back but he could only find three in the special drawer in the bureau, and it'd got the address label on it, too. She'd gone to Mass to get out of his way, and her mum told her to come round to my place as often as possible in these last ten days of the holidays, not to stand by her friend in her hour of need but so as not to provoke her father.

About three o'clock in the afternoon, the phone

rang again. I couldn't be bothered to answer it, but then I glanced through the French windows and saw Dad in a garden chair with the paper over his face and Mum out there too, weeding between the herbaceous what-nots with a flowery sunhat on her head. So I did go to the hall and answer it.

"Could I speak to Miss Robina Marquis, please?" said a female voice that I couldn't quite place.

"Um – it's Robina Marquis speaking. Miss Marquis." Suddenly, I'd placed the voice.

"It's Sister Horsley here, Severnside Hospital."

"Yes, Sister. What can I do for you?"

"It's my duty to check – I can't discharge a patient in his condition without knowing the address where he can be visited by the Social Services if necessary. Vernon Bridges is with me – "

Bridges – so that was his surname.

"He tells me you will provide himself and his father with accommodation until something more satisfactory is arranged. Is that correct?"

"Yes, that's perfectly correct," I said without a pause. "Could you tell him, please, to let himself in when he arrives. He has the key."

"Oh! Thank you, Miss – er... So you can assure me his father will be in safe hands?"

"I can indeed."

"Very well." Was she going to ask me for my address? I started making one up, ready: No. 3 Acacia... "Well, thank you, Miss Marquis. Goodbye."

"Goodbye." She put the phone down. So did I.

I sat down, and closed my eyes.

The bloody loon. He had it all worked out, didn't

he. "Rest," indeed. "Learning the lingo." He came here to see what he could get out of us. And he got what he wanted out of us – out of the Frys.

Surely they'll need passports? Yes – but you can get passports for Spain over the counter at the Post Office, can't you?

He's got three clear weeks at the villa, what with the Frys coming back early and old Harry not going after all. What about when the three weeks is up? He'll find somewhere. I know Vern.

You've got to give him credit. The cheek of it, the nerve, the ice-coolness. He only cares about one thing in life and that's his dad. He saw freedom for his dad and he took it. I opened the door, and in the last few minutes I've waved them through. *Beyond me into the starry night*.

I sat down. "EastEnders" had finished, and it was golf. It took me about quarter of an hour to stop trembling inside. Then I got an envelope and a couple of stamps out of Mum's drawer and went upstairs. I tore my last night's dream out of the exercise book, folded it together with Sekond Hand KarMart and Vern's dream, and wrote on a scrap torn from one of my old school books: "Keep on dreaming. So will I. No tracks please – leave the place neat." Then I put them in the envelope and stuck it down.

On the front I wrote *Mr Vernon Bridges*. I had to go to my bedroom and hunt through piles of old stuff till I found a letter from Cal at the villa last year about some other Don Juan, and I copied the address on to the envelope. Then I walked to the letter box to post it.

When I came back Mum was in the kitchen washing

the soil off her hands. She called, "Phew, it's hot. Want a cup of tea, darling? Been for a walk?"

"Yes, darling," I said.

TINKER'S CAREER
Alison Leonard

Tina was just a baby when her mother died. Now fifteen, she's determined to find out more about her. So, finding a photograph of her parents' wedding she sets out in search of her mother's family and the truth. But the truth – and with it the meaning of Tinker's Career – turns out to be even more devastating than she'd feared...

"Told at a heady pace with wonderful real, absorbing characters."
The Guardian

"Strong stuff."
The Times Educational Supplement

THE FIRST TIME
Aisling Foster

It's the summer term at William Stubbs Comprehensive and romance is in the air. Not for Rosa, though – style and painting are the loves of her life. But, as Rosa's sex maniac mum keeps telling her, there's a first time for everything. The important thing is to get it right...

"Brilliant and affectionate style-wars novel."
The Sunday Telegraph

SWEET WHISPERS,
BROTHER RUSH
Virginia Hamilton

Fourteen-year-old Tree has more than enough on her plate looking after her retarded older brother Dabney while her mother is away. Her emotional resources are tested to the full, though, when the ghost of Brother Rush appears, revealing some very disturbing truths about her family's past, which raise doubts about its future...

"A poignant story... The characters of Teresa and Dabney are superbly drawn... Totally captivating.'
The Times Higher Education Supplement

TIME PIPER
Delia Huddy

The door of the lab burst open. Something came out; something at floor level. It was lucky that Luke was not in the corridor or he might have been knocked out... Whatever it was came from the laboratory in a living torrent of bodies and swept down the corridor.

From the day he meets the beautiful, remote mysterious Hare, Luke's life is turned upside down. But what can be the connection between this strange lost girl and Tom Humboldt the brilliant inventor of a Time Machine? The answer, it seems, lies in the past...

"Very ingenious... A very good book."
The Standard

"Very perceptive ... not really sci-fi but a love story."
Peter Hunt, The Times Literary Supplement

SO MUCH TO TELL YOU
John Marsden

Scarred by her past, Marina has withdrawn into a silence. But then, set the task of writing a journal by her English teacher, she finds a new outlet for her thoughts and feelings and for exploring the traumatic events which have caused her distress.

"Beautifully written... A splendid read."
The Times Educational Supplement

Australian Book of the Year (Older Fiction) 1988

AWAITING DEVELOPMENTS

Judy Allen

A Whitbread Award Winner
Winner of the Friends of the Earth
Earthworm Award
Shortlisted for the Carnegie Medal

For some time, Jo's secret haven has been the beautiful garden of The Big House nearby. Now she is dismayed to learn that the site has been sold to a property developer, who plans to cover it with new flats and houses. To have any hope of stopping him, Jo must gain the support of her neighbours – most of whom are complete strangers. Naturally a shy girl, will she have the courage to make a stand?

This award-winning novel is a story that will stir the hearts of anyone concerned about the state of our environment.

"Full of humour and genuine feeling ... a highly attractive novel." *The Observer*

MORE WALKER PAPERBACKS
For You to Enjoy